The perfect p...

"You'd do anything for me?" Laurie interrupted. Enough was enough. The conversation was going in circles. Trent needed to see Tina's act for what it was. Then he would understand. And once he got a reality check, Laurie would make sure that Tina fell. Hard. And Trent would help bring her down. It was the least he could do.

"Anything," he said.

"Good." She leaned forward and planted a quick peck on his cheek. Easy as that, she had him. He would do anything she wanted. "So don't worry. Just play on my team. You trust me, don't you?"

"I trust you, Laurie." He pulled her close to him and brushed her hair away from her face, then kissed her on the lips.

Look for all the books in

#1 Julia
#2 Lucy
#3 Kari
#4 Trent

Available from HarperTrophy®
A Division of HarperCollins*Publishers*

Trent

Daniel Parker

HarperTrophy®
A Division of HarperCollinsPublishers

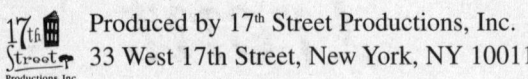 Produced by 17th Street Productions, Inc.
33 West 17th Street, New York, NY 10011

TRENT
Copyright © 2000 by 17th Street Productions, Inc., and Daniel Ehrenhaft.
Cover art copyright © 2000 by 17th Street Productions, Inc.

Harper Trophy® is a registered trademark
of HarperCollins Publishers Inc.

All rights reserved. No part of this book may be used or reproduced in any manner whatsoever without written permission except in the case of brief quotations embodied in critical articles and reviews. Printed in the United States of America. For information address HarperCollins Children's Books, a division of HarperCollins Publishers, 10 East 53rd Street, New York, NY 10022.

Library of Congress Catalog Card Number: 99-66684
ISBN 0-06-440812-4

To Jessica

Trent

Chapter 1

I'm doomed, thought Trent Rostand.

He knew it. And to make matters worse, he was the only one in homeroom who wasn't whooping it up. It was total pandemonium—like some kind of New Year's Eve blowout. Everyone was shouting. A boom box was cranked. Crumpled balls of paper were flying. Even Mr. Logan had his feet propped up on his desk.

But why not? This was the last day of school. The last *period* of the last day of school. With the possible exception of Christmas morning, it was supposed to be the high point of the year. Even birthdays didn't come close. Like his last birthday, for example. He had turned sixteen. It was a major milestone. An epic event. He should have been showered with all kinds of gifts people won at game shows—like a car, maybe, or a motorcycle, or a round-trip ticket to Tahiti. . . . Well, that was pushing it. But still. *Something* good. After all, his girlfriend had gotten a brand-new BMW, one of those slick two-seater convertibles that go from zero to sixty in about two seconds.

All he'd gotten was a new CD (by a band he didn't really like) and some clothes (stuff he would never wear). Oh yeah—and a book. A lousy book that he would certainly never read. Thanks, Dad. It was some sort of English literature anthology. About the size of a dictionary and equally as dull. Of course, if he'd actually *read* it instead of shoving it under his bed, he probably wouldn't be in the mess he was in right now. He wouldn't be poised for the biggest failure of his life. He wouldn't be on the verge of being yanked out of school by his father for poor grades in English, on the verge of losing *everything*.

That was Dad for you. He was devious that way. He'd give you something totally lame, and you wouldn't realize how much you needed it until your life was swirling around the toilet bowl. . . .

"Psst," a voice whispered at the next desk. "Trent. Earth to Trent. Can you hear me?"

He tried to smile. But even Laurie Penrow couldn't snap him out of his funk this time. And *that* was disturbing. Aside from being the most popular sophomore at North Conroe High (as if that weren't enough), Laurie was also the hottest. Hands down. It wasn't an opinion; it was a *fact*, like saying that the sky was blue. You could ask anyone. One glimpse of those long blond curls, those dark blue eyes, that body—a curvy bod ten years ahead of its time . . . whew. And Trent had been going out with her for four fantastic months.

"Don't tell me you're already getting nostalgic for the tenth grade," Laurie teased. "You still have half an hour left until the last bell rings. I mean, I'm going to miss Mr. Logan's polyester suits, too, but let's not get carried away."

Trent finally forced a weak smile. But Laurie's joking around only made him feel worse. He was going to lose her, wasn't he? Next year, when he was gone, Laurie would probably go out with a senior. Yup. Girls of Laurie's caliber *always* went out with seniors. Soon somebody else would take his place at Laurie's side. He anxiously ran a hand through his curly blond hair. Soon she'd forget all about him. . . .

"You're not still freaked about what your dad said, are you?" Laurie asked.

"I can't help it," Trent muttered. "He told me again at breakfast: If I don't get at least a C in English, he's going to send me to that military school, Stonybrook or whatever, and—"

"I thought it was a D," Laurie interrupted.

"Nope. He told me a C or better. Or I'm gone."

Laurie rolled her eyes. "And you actually believe him?"

"I have to, Laurie! Look, you don't know what my dad is like—"

"Shhh," Laurie whispered. She frowned, glancing around the room.

Trent sighed. So he was yelling. Big deal. The entire classroom was yelling. But then he saw the problem: a couple of girls (Tina What's-her-face and her redhead friend Susan Something) were whispering and staring at him and Laurie. Now he understood. He was embarrassing her. And if there was one thing Laurie Penrow couldn't stand, it was embarrassment. Why did she even care what other people thought? Those girls were probably just jealous of the fact that Laurie could easily be a Victoria's Secret model. Sometimes it drove him nuts how much Laurie worried about appearances. But whatever. He wouldn't let it bother him. Laurie was perfect in every other way. Besides, he had much more important things to worry about than his girlfriend's only character flaw.

"Sorry," he said.

"I just can't believe that your dad would put you in military school," she whispered. She leaned close to

him. "I mean, won't you get sent to the front lines if there's a war?"

"My dad would probably love that," Trent answered. "He'd say that it would teach me how to 'show some responsibility, show some initiative.' That's his big thing." He imitated the deep sound of his father's voice. "'Show some initiative, Trent. Get out there and kick some butt.'"

"Well, don't worry. You won't do that badly. I know you won't." She smiled. "English is your native language, remember?"

Right. He *should* be a good English student. It wasn't as if he had a bad vocabulary. He had a great vocabulary. He used real three- and four-syllable words in actual conversation, words like *voluptuous* and *caliber* and *devious*. Guys like Big Joe Biggs (the two-hundred-pound defensive end who sat on the other side of Laurie and took up half the classroom) probably couldn't even *spell* those words. But when it came to sitting down and slogging through the lame books that Mr. Logan assigned, really *concentrating* . . . well, his brain just couldn't hack it. The words on the page turned to mush. Inevitably he would get bored and turn to something good, a basketball mag like *Slam* or something cool like *Rolling Stone*.

"I'll tell you what," Laurie said with a wink. "Let *me* talk to your dad. I'm sure I could convince him to—"

"All right, people," Mr. Logan called from the front of the classroom.

A hush fell over the room.

"Let's settle down one last time. Your report cards have arrived."

Trent's stomach twisted. This was it. The moment he'd been dreading. Mr. Logan took a stack of cards from someone in the hall, then closed the door.

"Don't worry," Laurie whispered.

How can I not worry? he wondered. He'd heard rumors of what happened to kids at military school: First their heads were shaved, then their spirits were broken by steady abuse at the hands of sadistic drill sergeants . . . and gradually their former selves began to wither away until they disappeared altogether—replaced by brainless androids. He might as well just save his father the trouble and volunteer for a lobotomy. It would be a lot quicker. Probably a lot less painful, too.

"Sarah Abernathy," Mr. Logan called.

One by one, in alphabetical order, each student trudged to the front of the classroom.

"Mike Conrad . . . Susan Dwyer . . . Joe Feidelman . . ."

It wouldn't be long now. Trent's heart pounded. His

mouth was dry. He drummed his fingers on the desk. Nobody else had to endure this kind of torture, did they? It wasn't *fair*. Why was he the only kid at North Conroe whose father took parenting lessons from Napoleon?

"Laurie Penrow..."

She looked so cool and confident, swaggering up to the aisle to Mr. Logan, her blond curls tumbling off her shoulders. Of course she did. She had every reason to be cool and confident. She was, after all, practically a straight-A student. But even if she got straight Fs, her parents would never punish her. Nope. *Her* parents were normal.

Laurie's smile widened as she strolled back to her seat. Her triumph was plain for him to see, as clear as if it were being broadcast with an electronic billboard. He knew he should be happy for her. He really did. But right now, happiness for anyone was a long way off.

"Trent Rostand."

Oh no.

"Trent Rostand." Mr. Logan waved Trent's report card over his head.

Help. God, if you're up there, please let me have a C.

"Trent," Laurie hissed.

Okay, okay. His pulse pounded. Stonybrook wouldn't be *so* bad, would it? He'd probably get into great shape

there. At the very least, all the push-ups and calisthenics would be great for basketball. He was starting point guard on JV right now—but after a couple of years of military school, he would be N.B.A. material.

Yeah, right.

Summoning his strength, he stepped to the front of the classroom.

Mr. Logan handed over the card. He didn't seem very pleased.

And that's when Trent saw it. Right there, the last grade on the page, right under algebra.

English: C–.

No way. No way . . .

The funny thing was, he hadn't been *completely* convinced he would fail until this very moment. He'd felt pretty decent about his final exam. A part of him still believed that he was getting worked up for no reason at all, that he would somehow pull off a last-minute victory, just like he was always able to do on the basketball court. He had even pictured dancing back down the aisle right now, waving his report card over his head like a trophy. But no.

He shuddered. A strange weight seemed to fill his stomach, dragging it down. He was barely aware of returning to his seat.

"Trent?" Laurie murmured.

He couldn't tear his eyes from the grade.

She scooted over beside him. Her chair scraped on the floor. "Uh-oh," she said.

"I don't believe it," he croaked.

"Don't worry," she whispered. She put a hand on his shoulder.

He glanced up. *She* even looked freaked. Laurie Penrow *never* looked freaked. He winced.

"What am I gonna do?" he asked.

She chewed her lip for a moment. "I don't know," she said. "We have to figure out something. . . ."

Her expression frightened him. She clearly knew that he was a goner. So he'd better enjoy these final few minutes with her while he could. It was the last time he would ever sit next to his girlfriend in a North Conroe High School classroom.

"Wait!" she cried. She suddenly brightened. "I've got it! Of course. *Duh*."

"What?"

"You're going to go to summer school," she announced, staring him straight in the eye.

He waited for the rest. There had to be some kind of punch line.

"Don't you get it?" she said, laughing. "It's *perfect*.

Your dad is always telling you to show some initiative, right? So that's what you're going to do. You'll go home as soon as the bell rings—no, better yet, you'll call him at his office—and tell him that you tried your best, and you know that if you work a little harder, you can do better, and that you were so disappointed in *yourself* that you volunteered to take summer classes...."

You've gotta be kidding, he thought.

"What?" she asked defensively.

He shrugged. "I don't know, Laurie. I don't think he'd go for summer school. It's not really his style. He wanted me to get a job this summer."

"But that's just because he doesn't want you to sit around and do nothing," she insisted. "This way you're going to be *productive*. I mean, taking classes is a lot more productive than selling corn dogs at LotsaFunland, right?"

Laurie actually had a point. Trent *had* planned on getting a job at LotsaFunland—but only because that was what everyone else at North Conroe High did. Half the JV basketball team was going to be working there. The dilapidated old amusement park out on Route 40 was the only place anyone *ever* got jobs. It was basically a social endeavor, a way to hang out with people and still get paid for it. His father hadn't exactly been thrilled with the idea. He was smart enough to see Trent's motives for what they were.

But sitting indoors and reading Shakespeare all day . . . that was different. His father would be hard-pressed to argue with that.

"I'm sure he'll go for it," Laurie went on. "He's reasonable. A C-minus really isn't all that different from a C. If you're willing to sacrifice your whole *summer* just to bring your grade up that little bit, he's got to appreciate it."

Maybe she was right. Maybe his father would appreciate it. But when she'd said the words *sacrifice your whole summer,* Trent wasn't so sure if *he* appreciated it. It would essentially mean he'd have to take classes without a break for an entire *year*—starting now. Ugh. But anything was better than military school. Summer school for the rest of his *life* was better than military school.

Laurie must have sensed his reluctance because she patted him on the back. "Summer school really isn't that bad, especially when you consider the alternative. I think the classes only meet in the morning. In a way, it's almost *better* than having a job. You'll get to spend all your afternoons with me."

Hmmm. That was a very good point. He glanced at

her out of the corner of his eye. She was smiling seductively. The more he thought about the idea, the less crazy it sounded. Summer school would be a drag. But spending his afternoons lounging by the Penrows' pool, catching a few rays, enjoying the hot tub, with Laurie in her bikini . . .

"I'll give it a shot," he said finally. "I'll call him after school."

Laurie clapped. "Awesome. I know it'll work. You'll see. Trust me."

Tina

chapter 2

Fifteen more minutes. That was all she had left. Fifteen more minutes and she would be on summer break.

How depressing was that?

As far as Tina Vasquez was concerned, summer break just meant three whole months of some stupid and as-yet-to-be-determined job and three whole months of not seeing *him*.

What is my problem?

She knew she shouldn't be feeling sorry for herself. She should be ecstatic. It was summertime. And for one thing, there was a good chance she might find a really cool job. (Or at least a slim chance.) For another, *he* didn't even know she existed. She might as well be invisible as far as he was concerned. So what was the point in driving herself crazy over him?

There was no point. Right. She should view summer break as an opportunity. A big one. The next three months were going to mark a change. After all, her sixteenth birthday was coming up in July. A girl's Sweet Sixteen was her first step toward adulthood. It was time to grow up. It was time to stop obsessing over Trent Rostand. She was *way* too old to have a crush on someone. The cut-off age on crushes was around twelve. Everybody knew that. It was strictly a junior high thing. You stopped having crushes on boys in your homeroom right around the time you got your braces off.

Anyway, the only reason Tina thought about Trent so much was because she sat diagonally across from him. She was practically *forced* to think about him. To stare at him. To wonder what was going on inside that gorgeous head . . .

Jeez. This was pathetic. Summer break really *would* be a blessing.

Besides, she had already accepted that Trent Rostand was out of her league. *That* was painfully obvious. All she had to do was take one look at his girlfriend. Nobody at North Conroe was as beautiful as Laurie Penrow. Maybe Laurie sold her soul to Satan or something. And at the same time maybe she put a curse on Tina. That might explain why Laurie had blossomed, while Tina's thin frame seemed to have stopped developing in the sixth grade. Sure, she was taller, and she hadn't turned gawky or sticklike or anything like that, but she didn't get a few of the other attributes that Laurie had more than enough of. . . .

Tina rolled her eyes—just as a crumpled piece of notebook paper bounced on her desk.

> Argh! Will you please stop staring at you-know-who? Try to graduate the tenth grade with some dignity.
>
> Sincerely,
> L'il Orphan Annie

Tina had to smile. One thing about Susan Dwyer: No matter how lousy you felt, she could still make you step back and laugh at yourself. Maybe it was because Susan spent just as much time laughing at *herself*. Like the Annie joke. For some reason, Susan hated her bright red hair and freckles. Tina couldn't understand it. She would *love* to look like Susan: cute and bohemian, sort of like a grunge version of Raggedy Ann. Her hair was so cool. Tina's shoulder-length black bob, on the other hand, was distinctly *uncool*. It was cut in her own kitchen. By her own mother. Mom did a perfectly adequate job; Tina was

grateful—but there was no denying the amateurishness of a home haircut.

Oh, well. There was no point in sliding back into Sorry-for-Yourself Land. Tina flipped over the little piece of paper and pulled out her pen.

> I was not staring at him. If you want to know the truth, I've made up my mind. I'm completely over him. As God is my witness, I will never think of Trent Rostand again.

"Tina Vasquez," Mr. Logan yelled.

She jumped. The pen clattered to the desk. But Mr. Logan wasn't even looking in her direction. Tina rolled her eyes. He was just calling her name because it was time for her to get her report card. She sighed and crumpled the little piece of paper, then tossed it back to Susan and hurried up to the front of the room.

It was funny. Grades were about the last thing on her mind right now. But Tina never had any concerns gradewise. Report card time was always the *least* stressful time of year for her. Certain kids broke into a cold sweat when Mr. Logan called their names. But those were kids who viewed classes as unfortunate appointments on a busy social calendar. Tina was different. She got stressed about other things—like when she walked into the girls' room and the It girls suddenly stopped talking, then started again as soon as she left.

"Nice work, Tina," Mr. Logan said as he handed over the report card. He smiled at her over the rims of his glasses and leaned back in his chair. His brown polyester suit made a swishing noise. "You know, I never got a chance to tell you how much I enjoyed your essay on *Hamlet*. It was excellent. One of the finest essays I've ever seen from a student in this school. Really. If you don't mind, I'd like to use it as an example of essay writing in my summer school classes."

She smiled lamely. "Great. I don't mind at all—go ahead and use it."

Now she felt even *worse*. Why? Because a teacher was paying her a compliment? A list of nearly perfect grades sat in her hands. Her essay was being immortalized. This was cause for celebration. The problem was, every single bit of Mr. Logan's praise would make her *more* of an outcast—at least in certain people's eyes. Trent Rostand's, for one.

"Have a good summer, Tina. You've earned it," Mr. Logan said.

"Yeah, you too," Tina mumbled.

She stole a quick glance at Trent and Laurie as

she plodded back to her seat. *Look at them,* she thought, miserably. *What do they even talk about? I bet when Trent tries to say something remotely intelligent, Laurie switches the subject. I bet she starts babbling about shopping, or where her parents are taking her for vacation, or who's going to buy them beer for one of their raging parties....*

All right. Enough already. This kind of thinking would get her nowhere. It was time to start focusing on the *positive* things. So she wasn't Laurie Penrow. So she didn't go to parties every weekend or shop at Versace. She had her own scene. Her own friends. *Interesting* friends. Like Susan. Or the kids in North Conroe's Film Society. Or the kids who wrote for *Deep Ellum*—North Conroe's literary magazine—the school's unofficial club of misfits and artists.

The kids who read a lot and dared to think differently, even if it meant missing out on huge ragers and being voted prom queen.

Besides, for all she knew, Trent Rostand was a dolt. She'd barely said five words to him in her life. He never spoke in class. All intelligent signs pointed to the fact that Trent was all wrong for her. But she couldn't stop thinking about him. Why?

It had to do with what she'd seen out on the basketball

court—his fluidity, the way he improvised. It was like watching a dancer, a musician. Tina wasn't a huge sports fan, but she knew that a person couldn't play that way unless they were quick-witted. Unless they were creative, insightful. She could see the spark in his eyes. And she couldn't take her eyes off him. He *was* different from Laurie and the rest of the popular crowd. Wasn't he? Maybe if she learned more about basketball, she could—

Another crumpled ball of paper bounced on her desk.

Tina smirked. This was getting ridiculous. She glanced back at Susan. But Susan was staring off into space, deliberately twiddling her thumbs.

Major bulletin. Trent Rostand has to go to summer school. I just happened to overhear that he nearly failed English. Getting any ideas? As in, you still have to find a job? As in, being a summer school tutor pays six bucks an hour? (Yes, you can thank me later.) Picture this: You and the man of your dreams. An empty classroom. You're showing him the majesty of the English language. His heart is throbbing. I don't want to get any more graphic, but this is a golden opportunity. <u>Don't blow it.</u>

For a few seconds Tina stared blankly at her friend's scribbled words. Clearly Susan had lost her mind. Or maybe she had taken some kind of powerful drug as a way to celebrate the last day of school.

Susan kicked at her chair.

Tina frowned at her.

"Well?" Susan asked, raising her eyebrows.

"No way," Tina whispered, shaking her head.

"Why not?" Susan demanded.

Tina stole a furtive peek over her shoulder at Trent and Laurie. Her heart squeezed. They were kissing. *Kissing.* In the middle of homeroom.

"Don't pay any attention to that," Susan whispered. "Listen to me. It'll be perfect. See, this is a guy who can basically have any girl he wants. But he's never met anyone with that—"

"Shhh!" Tina hissed. She grabbed the bottom of her chair and scooted closer to Susan. "Stop talking so loud."

"Umm . . . Tina? I hate to break it to you, but nobody's listening. Nobody's paying any attention to us at all." Susan shrugged. "Not that this is unusual."

Susan had a point. The volume in the classroom had risen significantly. Mr. Logan was finished with the report cards. He was leaning back in his chair, staring at

the clock. Only two minutes remained until summer. For all intents and purposes, it *was* summer. About half the class was already standing, grouped in different little conversational circles.

"Just hear me out, okay?" Susan continued. "Basically, your life here at North Conroe can follow one of two paths. The first path is pretty much the one you've been on. You stare at a certain *very* popular, and *very* taken, guy from afar, you drool occasionally . . . yada, yada, yada. The second—the road less traveled, obviously—is that you seize the day, sign up to tutor him this summer, and see where fate takes you." Susan raised her eyebrows. "And maybe, just maybe, you find true happiness."

"Would that second path also be known as the yellow brick road?" Tina asked sarcastically.

"That's very funny," Susan deadpanned back. "Look, either way you get a full scholarship to Harvard, write a million-dollar screenplay, and marry some stallion who makes you-know-who look like dog city, okay? You can't lose."

Tina laughed. As ridiculous as it seemed, Susan was right: Tina really *couldn't* lose if she tutored Trent. She couldn't lose what she'd never had to begin with, right? It was a matter of logic. Worst-case scenario: Trent would turn out to be a complete idiot—a distinct possibility since he had to go to summer school in the first place. And Tina *did* need a job. Tutoring might be kind of fun. But it might be too late. Or even if she became a tutor, she might not tutor *him*. Then there was the issue of transportation. Her mother would have to drive her to school every single day. Tina wouldn't be getting her license until after her sixteenth birthday, which was still a good month and a half away. There were a lot of potential snags and what-ifs. On the other hand, school wasn't *that* far out of the way of her mother's commute—

Brrrriiiing!

The shrill sound of the bell tore through the room.

For a split second everyone was silent. Then all at once the entire class erupted with crazy clapping and hooting. Everyone else was up and out of their seats in a flash, on their way out the door. Except for Tina, who sat at her desk, still lost in her thoughts.

"Hey, Dorothy, the Wizard of Oz called. He wants to know if you're ready to click your heels and blow this joint?" Susan asked, looking at her with a big grin.

"You know what?" Tina said, grinning back at her.

"I'm gonna stick around. Need to swing by the office and ask about tutoring jobs."

Susan chuckled. "Didn't see *that* one coming."

And with that, Tina crumpled the note on her desk and headed for the garbage can, leaving tenth grade behind for good.

Laurie

The instant the final bell rang, Laurie Penrow yanked her boyfriend to his feet.

"You're going to call your dad right now," she informed him.

"But—"

"Now," she stated. They had to get away from this cheering. Neither of them had any reason to join in. Not yet, anyway. Also, cheering the end of the school year was so dorky—not to mention embarrassing. *Um, excuse me, folks? This happens every year, remember? We're not in the fifth grade, okay?*

"Whoa!" Trent stumbled behind Laurie as she snaked her way through kids and desks. "Hold up for a sec; can we at least say good-bye to—"

"I want to get this done so that we can start planning our Trent's-not-getting-a-flattop party," Laurie interrupted, nearly slamming into somebody on their way out the door. Correction: not *somebody* but *nobody*. The ultimate nobody, Tina Vasquez. Speaking of acting like a fifth grader . . .

Tina was blocking the only exit, hunched over the wastebasket, disposing of all the cutesy notes she and her chubby bosom buddy had been passing. It figured. Some people would *always* be stuck in elementary school, wouldn't they?

"Could somebody please move their rear end?" Laurie asked.

"What?" Tina said. "I—" She broke off when she looked up at Laurie. Her face reddened. Without another word she walked away.

Laurie shook her head. She suppressed a smile. *Poor Tina,* she thought. *When are you going to grow up? And get a real hairdo?* She really did feel sorry for the girl. Maybe someday she would get herself a makeover and a real salon cut. But maybe that was something Laurie didn't really want to have happen. Tina could be gorgeous if she put in a little effort—and just the sort of competition Laurie didn't want. . . .

But there were more important matters to worry about than Tina Vasquez. Laurie shook her head to clear her thoughts, and her grip tightened around Trent's hand. She dragged him purposefully into the hall, looking for a quiet spot amid the chaos. Dozens and dozens of kids were streaming past them, waving their arms and hooting like apes.

Ducking into an empty chemistry lab, Laurie took out her cell phone and handed it to Trent.

He took a deep breath. He flipped open the phone. His hands trembled.

"Well, here goes nothing," he muttered.

Laurie pulled him close and gave him a quick kiss on the lips. "Everything will work out," she told him. "Your dad's a smart guy. Trust me."

He nodded. "You're right."

She smiled. "Of course I am," she said. She smiled to herself as Trent punched in the number. Mr. Rostand *was* a reasonable man. He didn't want his only son to go to some fascist military academy. That was only a scare tactic. The move would be too traumatic for Trent. Even at a place like Stonybrook (or whatever it was called), little cliques must have already formed. The social hierarchy had already been established. Trent would have to start at the bottom. He was at the very top of the heap now. He couldn't handle such a drastic fall. Nobody could.

Besides, if *he* were yanked from North Conroe, where would that leave *her?*

Nowhere. Absolutely nowhere. She and Trent were a team, a unit. They *needed* each other. She didn't want to think about being without him. How could she face all their friends?

But everything was going to work out. . . .

"Hello, Dad?" Trent cupped a hand against his other ear to drown out the cacophony of departing students. "Yeah, it's me." He bit his lip and glanced at Laurie. "Well, that's kind of why I'm calling. . . ."

Laurie held her breath. She couldn't listen to this. It was too nerve-racking. She turned back toward the hall, losing herself in the whooping and hollering. Okay. She needed to chill. If Trent's dad *didn't* go for her plan, then . . . what? Her life would undergo some major changes. With Trent gone she'd be one of those tragic figures—a popular girl with no boyfriend. All the other eligible guys were taken. Who else was there? She wouldn't get invited anywhere. Parties would be out. (Who could she go with? Stand around by herself? Never!) The point was that she'd lose more than a boyfriend if she lost Trent. She'd lose her status. And she'd worked too hard to get where she was now to let that happen.

So as horrible and sickening as it seemed, she might have to . . . *No, no, no.* She could never do that. She could never look for someone to take Trent's place. She was panicking. Her mind was going places it shouldn't. Nobody at North Conroe could ever touch Trent, even if he wasn't here anymore. They would just have to deal with a long-distance relationship—

"Really?" Trent asked. "That's okay with you?"

She spun around. Trent was smiling. His eyes were wide.

Could it be?

Yes! Trent's old man had bought it!

"Yes, sir," Trent said, clearing his throat. He was struggling to contain his excitement, to sound sober and subdued—but he couldn't keep from smiling. "I understand. . . . No, I wouldn't want that, either. . . . Believe me, I won't let you down. . . . Thanks, Dad. Thanks a lot. I'll see you tonight."

He pressed the end button and folded the phone shut.

"Well?" Laurie said nonchalantly. There was no reason for Trent to know just how close she'd come to having a full-fledged nervous breakdown.

"He went for it," Trent whispered. His jaw was slack, as if he couldn't quite believe it himself. "He actually *went* for it." His smile widened. "He said exactly what you said he would: 'It's nice to see that you're showing some initiative, son.'"

Laurie shrugged. "I told you."

"You're a genius, Laurie. A *genius* . . ."

Before she knew it, he was sweeping her up in his arms and twirling her around like a rag doll. Her feet left the ground. *All right. Easy there, pal.* She laughed.

"I'm free!" he shouted. "I'm free! I'm—"

"Uh, Trent . . . I'm getting dizzy . . ." she whispered.

"Sorry, sorry." He set her gently back down on the floor.

Her head spun. She stumbled for a second, grabbing at the wall for support.

"So what do you wanna do now?" he asked breathlessly.

Laurie glanced out at the hall—just to make sure nobody had witnessed Trent's juvenile show of affection—then straightened her shirt.

"Go home and get your bathing suit," she instructed. "Then come over to my house for a little midafternoon celebration." She winked at him. "I've got a few loose ends to tie up."

He frowned. "What do you mean?"

"Summer school isn't the only trick I have up my sleeve," she said.

His eyes narrowed.

"You know Mrs. Witherspoon, in the registrar's office?"

she asked. "The one who gets all her fashion tips from Nick at Nite reruns?"

"I think I know who you mean, but . . ." He shook his head.

"She's in charge of summer school classes. And she happens to be one of my biggest fans." Laurie raised her eyebrows. "I just want to make sure she goes easy on my good friend Trent Rostand."

"Come on, Laurie." He moaned. "Don't do anything that'll get me into any trouble, all right? I'm on thin ice as it is. If my dad finds out you were involved . . ."

She put her hands on her hips, pretending to be offended. "Since when have I *ever* done anything that got you into trouble?"

He opened his mouth and closed it. Then he started laughing.

"Exactly," she said. "Now just be a good boy and go home, all right?"

By the time Laurie made her way to Mrs. Witherspoon's office, the school was all but deserted. Summer had officially arrived. The office was tucked away in a dark corner of the school building—by the exit nearest the Dumpster. It was a fitting spot. The only kids who ever had any reason to go there were the

ones who got dumped on: the troublemakers and burnouts.

Obviously Laurie didn't fit into either one of those categories. . . . But still, freshman year, she'd been known to cut a few classes and maybe even sneak a clandestine smoke out on the bleachers overlooking the football field. In the course of getting caught for such small vices, she'd gotten to know Mrs. Witherspoon—who, in addition to keeping track of every student's class schedule, also doled out various punishments.

But Laurie had won her over. Completely. By the end of their first encounter Mrs. Witherspoon was laughing, calling Laurie sweetheart, and tearing up the detention slip. Charming the old bat hadn't been hard, either. There was no big secret to the way the world worked. So long as you had good looks and class and knew how to use them, you could get what you wanted. You could even help your friends get what *they* wanted. And what harm was there in a little mutual back-scratching?

None, thought Laurie.

She hesitated outside the office door. For some reason, it looked especially forbidding: worn and weathered, with that opaque window that concealed the goings-on inside. Laurie hesitated in front of it. Was she doing the right thing? Of course. She needed Trent to stay in town, and to do that, he would have to make it through summer school. There was no way he could do it on his own. This was going to take some sweet talk and a little time, but she could do it. Conjuring up the sweetest smile she could manage, Laurie took a deep breath and raised her hand to knock . . . but then she stopped.

Somebody was in there already. She could hear the muffled sound of Mrs. Witherspoon's high-pitched, twittering voice.

". . . funny you should ask about him," she was saying. "I just got off the phone with his father, not ten seconds before you walked in."

"Really?"

Tina. Laurie instantly recognized the voice. Interesting. What was Tina doing with Mrs. Witherspoon? There was no way she could be in trouble. Geeks like Tina didn't *get* in trouble. Besides, it was the last day of school.

". . . can't help but be a little suspicious." Mrs. Witherspoon's tone was lighter now. "The moment he enrolls in Mr. Logan's summer school class, you appear at my door and volunteer to be his tutor. You and Trent Rostand wouldn't be conspiring together, would you?"

What? Laurie's eyes bulged. Tina and Trent? Conspiring together? *As if.* She took a step back, flabbergasted.

What was going on? How on earth did Tina know that Trent was enrolling in summer school? Laurie had come up with the idea less than fifteen minutes ago. And she hadn't *told* anyone. Even if she had, the *last* person she would tell would be . . .

"No, no," Tina said. "I just know that he's having trouble in English. . . ."

Okay. This was more than weird; this was *creepy*. She glared at the closed door. Somehow, in the past few minutes, Tina had learned all of Trent's secrets. Without even *talking* to him. But where could she have—

Homeroom.

Duh. Tina sat right behind Trent and Laurie, two rows back and two rows across, six feet away at most. The little freak must have listened in on their conversations. *Eww,* Laurie thought. Talk about gross. She suddenly felt like she was covered in a layer of slime. She'd never even considered the possibility that Tina was an eavesdropper. But now that she thought about it . . . Yes, every time she looked over her shoulder, Tina would be staring at her—then would quickly look away.

There was only one explanation.

Tina and Susan What's-her-face were plotting something. *That* was what all their stupid notes were about.

I bet she's going to sabotage Trent. It's the only reason

she would want to tutor him. She's going to make sure he flunks out.

Laurie chewed a thumbnail, shifting on her feet. This was not good. She had to find out exactly what Tina was up to.

She smiled.

Well. There was an easy way to do that, wasn't there?

Without another moment's hesitation Laurie marched back through the empty halls. Her determined footsteps echoed off the lockers and cinder-block walls. She'd never realized just how much Tina hated her. But now it was all becoming very clear. Tina was jealous of Laurie: of her popularity, of her boyfriend, of everything. And Tina thought she was pretty smart, too.

But Laurie was smarter.

In less than a minute she reached the deserted homeroom class. She opened the door and strode to the wastebasket.

Yuck. Do I really want to go through the garbage?

Luckily nothing *too* disgusting was in there . . . just a couple of papers, a few crumpled Kleenex—and right on top, the grand prize: Tina Vasquez's secret note.

Very gingerly Laurie plucked the note from the pile and unfolded it. Her breathing evened as she devoured the words. . . .

Well, well, well. She certainly hadn't been expecting *this*. No. This was enlightening, to say the least.

No wonder Tina was always staring at her and Trent. No wonder Tina blushed and ran off whenever the two of them came near. Laurie felt like a tremendous weight had been lifted. The sensation wasn't unlike what she'd experienced right after Trent had phoned his father.

Things were going to work out fine after all. Oh yes. Just fine.

Tina Vasquez had a crush on *her* boyfriend. And after reading this note, Laurie realized that Tina actually believed she had a chance.

With him. With Trent. Ha!

But in a way this was really the best of all possible circumstances. There was no *way* Trent would fail English now. No . . . everything was going to work out perfectly, just the way she wanted. Trent would ace the course.

Even better, Laurie would have a little fun this summer. She'd be able to teach Tina a few lessons about reality: namely, that she had no business trying to steal Trent away from her and scheming to meet him. Laurie laughed again. It was strange. She had actually been a little worried that the next three months were going to be totally boring. Until now she'd pictured one long, hot yawn fest—sitting by the pool and waiting around for Trent to finish work, day after day. But this summer school thing was going to spice it up. For sure.

She tucked the note into her pocket.

It was going to be a great summer after all.

Trent

I owe you, Laurie, Trent said to himself for about the hundredth time since he'd left school. *I owe you big time.*

He leaned back in the driver's seat, shifting the gears in his dad's black Jeep as it bounced up the winding roads lined with cacti and scrub brush. Early afternoon was always the hottest time of day in the hilly desert outside of North Conroe. The window was down. His T-shirt flapped in the wind. He'd been wearing the same foolish grin for the past hour. But he couldn't help it. He'd had another phone conversation with Dad when he got home—and the old man had actually told Trent that he was proud. "I'm proud of your decision to do this, son," he'd said. "It shows real foresight." Foresight. Incredible.

What had he ever done to deserve somebody as smart and beautiful as Laurie? How could he even *thank* her?

The Jeep bounced around a corner. The Penrows'

enormous split-level ranch home swam into view, sprawled across a vast lawn that was adjacent to stables and a riding ring. The lush green grass always looked a little fake—probably because there wasn't another lawn for miles. Twenty-four hours a day, sprinklers were whirling and uniformed gardeners were tending to it, making sure it stayed the same bright, bright green. A few horses stood around the ring, munching on sheaves of hay.

Even though Trent had come here almost every single day for the past four months, he still couldn't get over how amazing Laurie's house was. He sighed as he downshifted and turned into the driveway. Who else had a lawn in the middle of the desert? The Penrows literally lived like royalty. But hey, if *his* father owned half of Texas, he'd probably live like royalty, too.

Trent jerked to a stop.

The moment he cut the engine, Laurie burst out the front door. She came running down the long walk to the driveway—in her bikini, no less. She'd obviously been out by the pool for a while. Her long, browned legs glistened with suntan lotion. She was wearing dark glasses.

"Today is your lucky day, Trent Rostand!" she called.

No kidding, he thought. He hopped out of the Jeep

and closed the door. Just looking at Laurie made him feel lucky. He could drop dead right now and *still* be lucky.

She rushed right up and kissed him on the lips.

He nearly fell backward. "Well, hello to you, too."

"That's just my way of congratulating you," she said casually. "You know, for getting an A-plus in English this summer."

He blinked at her. "Um . . . don't I actually have to go to classes first? I think I heard that somewhere."

She flashed a secretive grin, then took his hand and began to lead him down the dusty path around the side of the garage to the pool. "Details, details," she said. "The point is, your worries are behind you. It's time to start enjoying yourself."

He knew that smile of hers. It was dangerous. "All right, Laurie, what did you do?"

"Me?" she asked, pretending to be surprised. She let go of him as they walked down a short flight of stone steps to the patio. "I didn't do a thing. Somebody else did."

"Who? Your imaginary friend? A little birdie?"

"Please." Laurie stretched herself out on a cushioned recliner by the edge of the massive, oval-shaped pool. It was even hotter back here than it was out front. Beads of sweat formed on Trent's forehead. His eyes wandered toward the water. Maybe he should change into his bathing suit.

"So?" he prodded, glancing back at her. "Are you going to tell me what happened?"

"Do you know who Tina Vasquez is?" she asked.

He thought for a minute. Should he? Tina Vasquez . . . Tina Vasquez . . . No, he was pretty sure he didn't know anybody with the first name Tina. Well, there was that girl who was always giggling and passing notes in homeroom. But why would Laurie mention *her?*

"Is she that girl who sits behind us in homeroom?" he asked tentatively.

Laurie took off her glasses and looked him straight in the eye. "Bingo." She sat up straight, smiling again. "*She's* going to be your English tutor this summer."

Trent shook his head, baffled. "I don't get it. How do you—"

"She volunteered for the job," Laurie interrupted matter-of-factly. "She wants to get you alone in a classroom. She's hoping to spark a little romance."

All right. Time to rewind. Laurie wasn't making any sense.

"Tina Vasquez has a major crush on you," Laurie declared. "She happened to eavesdrop on our little talk

about grades today. She heard you were going to take summer school classes in English—so as soon as the final bell rang, she ran off to Mrs. Witherspoon's office to get in on the action."

He gaped at her. Then he started laughing. "How do you *know* all this?" he asked.

She pointed toward the little side table next to the recliner. "I have it in writing."

In writing? Trent stepped forward and followed Laurie's finger. Tucked under an empty glass was a crumpled scrap of paper. No way. She couldn't be serious. He snatched up the note, then began to read out loud: "'Major bulletin. Trent Rostand has to go to summer school. . . .'"

His voice trailed off. *Whoa.* Laurie wasn't kidding. He tore through the rest of it in silence. This was crazy. (Although it was pretty flattering, he had to admit.) But didn't Tina Vasquez know that he had a girlfriend? She *must* know—everybody knew that he and Laurie were a couple. Besides, she sat right behind him and Laurie. So why would she try to become his tutor? He probably hadn't ever spoken to her in his life.

"See what I mean?" Laurie asked, closing her eyes and leaning back in the chair.

He shook his head, gazing over the words again.

"Wow," he muttered. He didn't really know what else to say. He put the note back on the table and sat on the recliner beside her.

"The note is right, you know," Laurie said. "This could be a golden opportunity."

"What do you mean?"

"Think about it. This girl wants something. To put the moves on you. You want something, too. To avoid wearing a green uniform for the next two years." She winked at him. "And now you can both get what you want."

His blue eyes narrowed. "I'm not sure I'm following you. How can *she* get what she wants?"

"She can't," Laurie said. "But if she *thinks* she can, you'll have a much better chance at getting a good grade, right?"

He shook his head. Once again he found himself laughing. Laurie was smart, but sometimes she could get devious. "You want me to string this girl along? Come on, Laurie. That's low."

Laurie shrugged. "Whatever. She wants to steal you from me. That's what this whole tutoring thing is about. Read the note again. If you ask me, that's *lower* than low."

"Oh, come on," Trent teased. "Isn't that a little dramatic? If you ask *me,* the best way to deal with this is to ask Mrs. Witherspoon to put me with another tutor.

That way I can concentrate on English instead of concentrating on having to explain to somebody that I already have a girlfriend." He glanced at her out of the corner of his eye. "An amazingly brilliant and sexy girlfriend, I might add."

"Don't try to flatter me," she said with a smirk.

"I'm not. I'm just telling the truth."

She sighed, but her smile softened. "I'll tell you what. Let's make a deal. Let her be your tutor for one day. If she's all over you and you can't concentrate, ask for another one. But if she makes your life easier, go for it."

Trent started smiling, too. Why was it impossible to say no to Laurie Penrow? Of course, she wasn't asking him to do something totally unreasonable. At the very least he could set this Tina person straight. It was only fair. To her *and* to Laurie.

"Hey, Laurie? Can I ask you something?"

"Sure."

"Where did you *find* that note, anyway? Was it in the garbage or something?"

"Eww, Trent, that's *gross!*" she cried. "Of course not. It fell out of her bag as she was leaving Mrs. Witherspoon's office. She must have left her zipper open."

Trent blinked. That was pretty coincidental. Almost *too* coincidental. Maybe for some bizarre reason Tina

wanted Laurie to find the note. But why? It was so embarrassing....

"What's the matter?" Laurie asked.

"Nothing." He took a deep breath and shook his head. He was just paranoid. He was really crazy about Laurie, but sometimes he just wasn't sure how much he could trust her. She was used to getting things her way. And sometimes it seemed like she would do anything to make sure that happened.

"Look," Laurie said, breaking into his thoughts. "This is really the best-case scenario. Either way you can't lose, right?"

"Right," Trent agreed. He began to relax. That was what he loved most about Laurie: her ability to turn any situation around for the best. He reached over and ran a hand through her golden curls. It was a good thing *one* of them had brains, wasn't it?

Tina

chapter 5

<u>Susan Dwyer's Four-Step Program to Landing the Guy of Your Dreams</u>

1. Always look him in the eye. (If you're feeling brave, bat your lashes.)
2. Laugh at his jokes, no matter how awful.
3. Make him feel smart. Ask him about basketball and pretend to be really, really interested. For practice on dealing with boring conversations, I'd recommend spending five minutes with my stepfather. (Warning: May cause brain damage.)
4. When he's not looking, jump on him. (Only use if 1, 2, and 3 don't work.)

Nice. Tina shook her head. Was this supposed to make her feel better? Susan must have slipped the note into her book bag last night while they were hanging out in Tina's kitchen. Tina could *kill* her.

What am I doing?

She sat very still and straight in the empty, silent classroom. Her heart pounded. Her fingers were moist. This chair was too hard. It was too hot in here....

She was so stupid for letting Susan talk her into this. Just *being* in school on a Monday in the middle of June was enough of a nightmare. Only a few other kids were around, along with a few teachers and staff: a handful of people spread out and isolated in various classrooms like hermits. Being in a school in the summertime just wasn't right. The atmosphere was so *weird*—as if she'd stepped into an alternate dimension or ghost town. Or a prison. Yes, at the moment North Conroe High felt distinctly prisonlike.

And where was Trent, anyway?

Okay, he wasn't that late; it was only five past nine. Unfortunately *she'd* been here for almost half an hour. Her mom had no choice but to drop her off extra early. It was the only way she could still manage to make it to *her* job on time—which meant, of course, that Tina could look forward to a whole summer of the same torture. Yup. Fantastic. Every single morning for the next two months she would sit by herself in a classroom for half an hour and fret about Trent Rostand's impending arrival.

Add to that another half hour at home, fretting about what clothes to wear. She'd tried on almost everything in her closet. The idea was to look great without looking like she had worked at it too hard—sort of the look that Laurie managed to pull off every day. But without the designer clothes and killer bod, it wasn't happening. So instead she had opted for the usual summer wardrobe: baggy jean shorts and a cotton tank top. At least she chose a faded blue tank, one that Susan said set off her honey-colored skin.

The hair? There wasn't much she could do with it: straight and sleek to her shoulders, it was dark, like her eyes, and, Tina thought, very boring, not long and sexy like Laurie's. Tina thought again about what Susan had said last night: "Girls like Laurie are all over the place. You're special: smart and funny, and even though you don't want to believe it, you're more classy looking than Laurie could ever hope to be."

But staring down at her faded jeans, Tina didn't feel classy. She almost wished her mom hadn't been so thrilled about this job.

For such a ludicrous, spur-of-the moment idea it had fallen into place without a single hitch. Her mom

thought that tutoring was great; Mr. Logan thought it was great; Mrs. Witherspoon thought it was great (after being convinced that Tina and Trent were *not* conspiring together) . . . and now here she was, about to spend a full hour with him.

Wasn't the whole point of this summer to move beyond Trent Rostand? Didn't she want to forget about her crush on him?

Maybe she would, though. After all, she was going to have to tutor a bunch of other students in the afternoon as well. Maybe she'd meet some sweet, sensitive guy in the afternoon and form a *real* relationship.

Sure. The chances of that happening were about one in eight zillion.

She stared down at Susan's note, sitting on top of her worn paperback copy of *The Taming of the Shrew*. To top it all off, Mr. Logan had assigned Trent to read a play about a guy who disguises himself as a tutor to be with the woman he loves. It was just a little too close to real life, even though the genders were reversed. But Tina probably wouldn't be able to talk about it without turning bright red. . . .

Remember, you're doing this to prove that you don't have a crush on him, she told herself. It had become her personal mantra. *You're doing this—*

The door flew open.

"Hey. Sorry I'm late."

So much for the mantra. Trent Rostand was here. *Now.* She couldn't move. She stared at him as he casually slung his book bag onto the floor and slumped into the desk beside her. He flashed a quick smile. She gave her best effort at a smile back. He had to be even more gorgeous than ever, didn't he? He'd gotten a tan. His blue eyes glistened in the morning sunlight. He was wearing a baggy T-shirt and khaki shorts that hung perfectly from his tall, muscular frame. . . .

Stop staring at him! Say something!

He extended a hand. She forced herself to shake it. His hands were big, and her little hand was lost in his for a moment. A little shiver went up her arm, and she felt warm. Was she blushing already?

"I'm Trent," he said. "Mrs. Witherspoon probably told you."

"Yeah. She did. I'm Tina."

"Nice to meet you," he said. "Officially, I mean. We're in the same homeroom class. Mr. Logan's actually going to be my summer school teacher."

"Yeah. I know. Uh . . . it's nice to meet you, too."

He started rummaging through his book bag. "So, um, I don't really know what we're supposed to do

here. . . ." He pulled out a notebook and put it on his desk. "I think you're gonna have to show me the ropes."

Tina nodded, swallowing. "Yeah, I guess the basic idea is that—" She broke off. Panic seized her. Susan's "instructions" were still sitting right on top of her desk. She shot a quick glance at Trent. He was digging in his bag for a pencil. Without taking her eyes off him, she opened *The Taming of the Shrew* and shoved the note inside it. That was it: She would definitely have to kill Susan.

Trent glanced up. "What's the basic idea?"

"Uh . . . well, to be honest, I'm not really sure." Tina couldn't even remember what they'd been talking about. *Smooth, Tina,* she thought. *Real smooth.*

He laughed. "It's nice to know that the tutor is as confused as the tutoree."

"No, no. I mean, uh—uh . . . I think that we're supposed to talk about your assignments—you know, before you go to class," she stammered. "You have class at ten, right?"

He nodded.

This was ridiculous. Why would she ask such a stupid question? Of *course* he had class at ten. That was the way summer school worked: tutoring from nine to ten, then classes from ten to twelve-thirty, then more tutoring until five. She was babbling. "It's just that, this being the first day of summer school and all, you don't have any assignments yet," she said quickly, hoping she didn't sound as nervous as she felt. "So as far as today goes, I'm not sure what we're supposed to do."

Trent leaned back and grinned. "Well, we could always stare at the clock for an hour. That's pretty much what I usually do in class, anyway."

Tina laughed.

Suddenly she felt relaxed. The laugh wasn't phony or forced. Incredibly enough, it was natural. He'd cracked a joke, and she'd found it funny. It was perfectly normal. This wasn't so bad. *She* was making it a lot worse by getting so stressed. From what she could tell so far, Trent wasn't a god, or a jerk, or an idiot . . . or *any* of those things. He was just a guy. A very handsome guy, yes—but nothing more.

"You know what?" he said abruptly. "I think maybe I should go talk to Mrs. Witherspoon about getting another tutor. I mean, it's just—"

Tina interrupted. "You can't be bored already. . . ." She tried to keep the hurt out of her voice. She *wanted* to be Trent's tutor. Clearly the best way to get over her crush on him was to spend time with him. Then she would get to know him as just a *guy* and not some silly fantasy. Besides, *The Taming of the Shrew* was one of her favorite plays. Helping him with it would be a cinch.

"It's just that . . . um, I'm not really a morning person," he mumbled uncertainly. "I don't know if I can deal with getting up this early. I might want to switch to an afternoon tutor."

Tina smirked. "If you're not a morning person, how come you're so hyper in homeroom every morning? Are you giving up Fruity Pebbles or something?" She couldn't believe she was having a normal, if somewhat goofy, conversation with Trent Rostand.

He laughed. "That's different. Goofing off doesn't require any thinking. Thinking is where I have the problem." He waved his hands at the classroom. "Why do you think I'm here?"

"Maybe because goofing off is also easier than reading Shakespeare," Tina proposed, feeling herself relax. "Believe me, I can tell already that you don't have any trouble thinking."

His brow grew furrowed, but he was smiling.

"Besides, all that stuff about being a morning person is just an excuse that smart people like you use to get out of doing anything before noon."

"Touché," he said.

Tina laughed. He was pretty sharp. Tutoring him

might actually turn out to be a lot of fun. It already *was* fun.

"Why don't I tell you a little about the first book you're supposed to read for Mr. Logan's class?" she suggested. "Sound good?"

Trent nodded, but he seemed reluctant. His eyes darted to the clock above the door. "Um, okay, I guess. . . ."

"Come on. I mean, we're *here,* aren't we? We might as well do something." She slid the book toward him across the desk—making sure the weight of her hand prevented Susan's note from slipping out. "Have you ever heard of this play?"

He blinked. His expression was mischievous. "Uh, well . . . I've known a shrew or two. And I saw *Shakespeare in Love* with my parents. Does that count?"

"It's a start. What did you think of it? Did you like it?"

"Not as much as my parents did," he mumbled. "I mean, *Gwyneth Paltrow* was all right. It's just that I didn't get a lot of the jokes. Some of it was funny, though."

"Well, believe it or not, *The Taming of the Shrew* is funny, too," she encouraged.

He eyed the book dubiously. "Really?"

She rolled her eyes at him in exaggerated frustration. "Yeah. Trust me. I like a good laugh as much as the next girl, and this is funny stuff."

He grinned. "Well, *that's* nice to know," he said.

"It reads really fast, too," she added.

"For *you*, maybe." He sighed, shaking his head. "See, this is the whole problem. I'll start something by Shakespeare—fully meaning to read it, knowing it must be good because people have been reading it for four hundred years—but then I'll hit some hard words or some line that doesn't make any sense . . . and I'll just lose interest. You know?"

"But that's where I come in," Tina reassured him. "Anytime you have trouble with a passage, underline it and we'll talk about it. You can even give me a call at home if you want—" She stopped. That didn't sound like she was hitting on him, did it? Because she *wasn't*. It was a totally innocent suggestion.

"I can call you at home?" he asked, sounding shocked. "Wow. That's so nice of you."

She looked down at the book. "Well, that's what I'm here for—to help. You know?"

"Okay. Um . . . but can I ask you something? There wouldn't happen to be a movie version of *The Taming of the Shrew*, would there?"

She burst out laughing again. "Maybe, but it would be pretty old. There aren't any of those modern interpretations of this one, if that's what you're asking, like that *Romeo & Juliet* with Leo DiCaprio and Claire Danes. Not that I know of, anyhow. And I'm in the Film Society. I think I've seen more movies than Roger Ebert." Tina realized she was rambling, but she seemed powerless to stop her mouth from going on. "Anyway, in my opinion, reading Shakespeare's better than watching it. Sans Gwyneth Paltrow, of course."

"I'll take your word for it," he answered. "So what's this play about?"

"It's pretty much about this guy, Petruchio, who marries this really harsh girl, Kate. He manages to change her ways. In the end she's really nice, a total sweetheart. But there's a lot of cool stuff that happens in between. The whole play is actually a play within a play."

He nodded. His eyes seemed distant.

"Uh-oh," she joked. "Earth to Trent."

"No, no, it's just that . . ." His voice trailed off. "Forget it. I'm sure you don't want to hear about the stupid problems of some complete stranger."

Tina bit her lip. Stupid problems? Was it her imagination, or was Trent Rostand on the verge of confiding in her about something?

"Sure, I would," she prompted. "Anyway, you're not a complete stranger. We shook hands, remember?"

He managed a little half smile. "Yeah, I guess you're right."

Hmmm. He was obviously holding something back. But she didn't want to push him. She didn't want to act nosy. "What's wrong?" she ventured.

"Nothing. It's just . . . uh, I really want to do well in summer school," he said.

"Who says you won't?" she asked.

"I don't know," he mumbled. He slumped back in his chair and smiled again. "It doesn't matter. I'm sorry. Forget it."

She shrugged. "No problem. But I want you to know—if it makes your life easier, you can just think of me as your tutor *and* your shrink."

He glanced at her out of the corner of his eye. All at once he started cracking up.

"You know, I don't think this morning stuff is gonna be so bad after all," he said.

Tina nodded. She laughed along with him. She *knew* it wasn't going to be bad. Today marked a milestone. She was officially over Trent. She was no longer the same old Tina, the shy girl who passed notes in class and pined for a perfect stranger. She was breaking free of her old ways. Maybe she had allowed herself to become a tutor because she'd secretly dreamed that Trent would fall for her, but that was all in the past. In tutoring Trent, she was going to become his *friend*. Nothing more.

Her life was changing. And it was changing for the better.

Laurie

chapter 6

The hot sun was at its highest point in the sky—the best hour for tanning—when Laurie heard the faint rumble of Trent's Jeep in her driveway. The car door slammed. A smile spread across her face. *Finally,* she thought. She'd been sunbathing by the pool for what seemed like *years,* waiting and waiting. . . . She would really have to find some way to occupy her mornings. Dealing with this kind of suspense was going to give her high blood pressure. She kept imagining that Tina had quit, or that she was assigned to tutor someone else at the last minute—or that Trent had decided to be honest and to do all his work himself, in which case he probably *would* end up going to military school. . . .

Footsteps shuffled down the patio steps.

Laurie kept her eyes closed until Trent was standing right beside her.

"Hey, there," he whispered. "You're not asleep, are you?"

She squinted up at him, shielding her face from the sun with her hand. "Hey, there, yourself, summer school boy. So how was the first day?"

"It was . . . well, it was *weird*," he muttered.

Uh-oh. Laurie propped herself up on her elbows and peered at him closely. *That* didn't sound very promising. "What do you mean?"

Trent sighed and sat down on the recliner beside her. He shook his head. "I went in there this morning—you know, to see if I could deal with Tina . . . and it went great. I mean, I think she's really gonna help me out with English."

"So what's the problem?"

"It's just . . ." His voice trailed off. "I was expecting something different."

"Like?" Laurie asked.

He shook his head again, staring down at the ground. "I don't know." He laughed suddenly. "I guess I was expecting there to be a little tension or something. You know, because Tina has a crush on me or whatever. But I don't get it. She just acts normal around me. I don't think she likes me that way. And to be honest, I don't know if she even did to start with."

"What are you talking about?" Laurie asked, baffled. "You saw the note."

"I know." He looked up at her. "Maybe we just got the wrong idea from it. Anyway, Tina didn't even write it. That other girl . . . Susan What's-her-face did."

Something about his tone struck her as odd. "How could we get the wrong idea? What happened?"

He shrugged. "Nothing. And that's just it. We got along really well. She's really easy to talk to."

Easy to talk to? He had to be playing a joke on her. This was much too strange. There was no *way* Trent could enjoy talking to Tina Vasquez.

"Well, the point is, you were right as usual," he said with a smile. He stretched out on the recliner and closed his eyes, turning his face toward the sun. "It would have been dumb to switch tutors. Tina is going to be great."

All at once Laurie felt annoyed—and she wasn't even sure why. "Of course she's going to be 'great,'" she said. "She wants you to fall for her."

Trent opened his eyes and glanced at her. "Come on, Laurie. I'm telling you, the girl is totally normal and nice. She's not interested in me. Just drop it, okay?"

"That's what she wants you to think for the time being," Laurie said. "Don't you get it? She's pretending

not to be interested in you because that will make *her* more interesting. She doesn't want to come on too strong."

He started laughing. "I don't know, Laurie. That sounds kind of far-fetched."

For some reason, his laughter only made her *more* annoyed. It seemed like Trent was deliberately playing dumb about Tina. And now that Laurie thought about it, the idea of their being alone in a classroom every day for an hour sounded a lot less appealing than it once had. Who would have thought that he would enjoy her company? Laurie shook her head. There was no way she was going to allow Tina to play games with her boyfriend and not do something in return. *She* was the one who should be calling the shots, who should be in control. This whole summer school idea was hers in the first place.

"You obviously don't know much about girls," she finally said.

"I guess I don't," he mumbled. "I sure don't know why you're mad at me right now."

"I'm not mad."

"Good. Because all I did was follow your advice." He closed his eyes again and stretched out on his back. "And even if Tina *does* like me, that's her problem—not mine."

Hmmm. Trent still wasn't getting it, was he? This *was* his problem. People like Tina couldn't go around thinking they were equal to people like Laurie—she had worked too hard to get where she was to have someone like Tina come along and weasel her boyfriend away. People like Tina needed to learn their place in the world. And in some ways, Trent needed to learn *his* place, too. Tina was stringing him along, and he didn't even know it. And *that* was not a set of circumstances that Laurie was prepared to accept.

"Do you want me to switch tutors?" Trent asked in the silence. "That's fine with me."

"No," she said. She nodded to herself. An idea was forming in her head. Ah, yes. The gears were meshing. The electricity was pumping. The machine was whirring to life. Her *new* plan would make the old one seem third-rate by comparison.

It wasn't enough for Trent simply to use Tina to get a good grade. No. Soon little-miss-nerd would learn her place in the grand scheme of things. She would find out that losers like her don't mix with people like Trent Rostand.

Besides, Laurie wasn't about to sit back and let her summer pass her by without a little fun.

"In fact . . . I want you to tell Tina that we broke

up. I want you to tell her that you're single now."

Trent's eyes popped open, and he sat up. "What?"

She smiled. "You heard me."

"Why would I want to do that?"

"So that you'll get a good grade, Trent," she said. "We've already been over this."

"I know, but . . . look, that plan is no good. Tina isn't interested in me, whether she thinks I'm single or not. I'm just going to have to study this summer—there's no easy way out of it, no matter how much you want things to go your way."

Laurie glared at him. "This isn't about getting my way. This is about helping you. I think you're forgetting that I saved your butt last week. If you'll recall, I was right then, and I'm right now. You'll just have to trust me on this."

He frowned at her. "What's this about, Laurie? I mean, *really*. Do you have something specific against Tina Vasquez?"

"Only that she's trying to move in on my boyfriend," Laurie answered. Her tone hardened slightly—just to let him know that she wasn't kidding around. "And in answer to your first question, this is about keeping you *out* of basic training and *in* North Conroe, where you belong."

"But you've already *done* that," he said. His voice

rose slightly. "And I'm more grateful to you than you'll probably ever know, but I still don't—"

"So you won't mind playing a little joke on Tina," Laurie interrupted. "Just think of it as a favor to me. It's girl stuff, Trent."

Trent shook his head. His forehead was creased. "I don't know...."

Laurie sighed. "Trent, the more Tina does for you, the more time *we'll* be able to spend together, right? I'm doing this for us. So *we* can have fun, right?"

"I guess," he said uncertainly.

"Good." She lay back down and turned her attention to deepening her tan.

Trent laughed softly.

"What now?" Laurie was losing her patience.

"Nothing. It's just . . . Never mind."

"Never mind *what?*" she asked. "Tell me."

"You might get angry."

"Telling me that isn't making me *less* angry," she muttered.

"Well . . . it's just funny," he said. "The first thing I have to read for Mr. Logan's class is *The Taming of the Shrew*, this Shakespeare play. It's about this guy who marries this girl who's kind of harsh. And in the end she mellows out."

She snickered. "What is that supposed to mean?"

"I don't know," he mumbled. "Nothing. Forget it."

"No. You said it." She shot him a cold stare. "What?"

"Maybe we should *all* just mellow out a little bit. It's summer, you know?"

Her face darkened. He actually felt sorry for Tina Nobody, a geek whom he'd never given a moment's thought before today. Just because Tina had taught him a little bit about Shakespeare, he suddenly thought she was some kind of saint? It was absurd. He didn't know her at all, and he didn't owe her any charity. He owed Laurie, in case he'd forgotten. What did he care if Tina's feelings got hurt? Everybody at North Conroe played mind games with each other—Tina included. Besides, Laurie was doing this mostly for *him*.

"Excuse me if I have a hard time being mellow," she said. "I'm just busy trying to make sure my boyfriend doesn't get shipped off to some military prison. Remember?"

"Of course I remember!" he yelled. "I just want to know why we're fighting, you know?"

Laurie swallowed. That was a good question. Why *were* they fighting? She didn't want to fight with Trent. All she wanted was to put a little excitement into an otherwise boring summer, to set the stage for at least another two years of bliss. . . .

"Look, I'm sorry," Trent murmured. He swung his legs over the side of the recliner and leaned close to her, taking her hands in his. "I know I wouldn't even be sitting here right now if you hadn't come up with the summer school idea. But if you saw what happened today, you probably wouldn't want to—"

"You'd do anything for me?" she interrupted. Enough was enough. The conversation was going in circles. Trent needed to see Tina's phony I-don't-even-like-you act for what it was. Then he would understand. And once he got a reality check, Laurie would make sure that Tina fell. Hard. And Trent would help bring Tina down. It was the least he could do.

"Anything," he said.

"We're a team, aren't we?" she persisted.

"Of *course* we are," he whispered.

"Good." She leaned forward and planted a quick peck on his cheek. Easy as that, she had him. He would do anything she wanted. She had to admit, guys were pretty predictable—even guys as awesome as Trent. "So don't worry. Just play on my team. You trust me, don't you?"

"I trust you, Laurie." He pulled her close to him and brushed her hair away from her face, then kissed her on the lips.

Trent's lips were amazing, and Laurie knew she

should forget everything else and lose herself in the moment. But her mind was still focused on Tina. Yes... on Tina and her impending downfall. Most of all, Laurie was filled with the excitement of teaching Tina a lesson that had been many years in coming. *That* was what would make the long, hot summer months worthwhile. She'd even come up with a name for her little scheme: Operation Sweet Sixteen.

Trent

chapter 7

Trent hesitated in the hall outside the classroom and peered through the cracked glass of the door. The morning sunshine streaming through the windows was *way* too bright. Man, he was groggy. He'd never get used to waking up this early in the summertime.

Tina, on the other hand, was clearly wide awake. She sat straight at one of the desks, reading . . . completely oblivious to the surprise that awaited her.

He chewed his lip for a moment. It was strange: Tina looked kind of pretty today—dressed in another pair of jean shorts and a colorful T-shirt, with her glossy dark hair in pigtails, tiny barrettes framing her face. Pretty, but that wasn't exactly the wardrobe he would imagine for a girl who was secretly plotting to ruin a perfect stranger's relationship with her boyfriend. She looked more like she belonged in a Britney Spears video.

Could it be Laurie was wrong about her?

Maybe. Yesterday he'd almost told Tina that he wanted to switch tutors because he'd heard that she liked him. But he didn't want to embarrass her. And he had to admit . . . he'd been a little disappointed that she *didn't* like him—at least not romantically. Not that he was attracted to her or anything. She wasn't really his type; he went for blondes, like Laurie. Tina was the exact opposite—tall, thin, brunette. Sure, she was attractive, but not his type. Not at all. Still, it was always nice to know that somebody liked you. . . .

Why do I even care so much?

He shook his head. Tina's feelings didn't matter. At least, not compared to Laurie's. He couldn't second-guess himself. Even if Laurie's plan was a little on the harsh side, he couldn't back down. He had to prove to Laurie that she was the most important person in his life, that he'd never be able to repay her for keeping him at North Conroe High and *out* of military school. If today's trick was the only way he could do it, then fine. Besides, why should he even *care* about Tina Vasquez? He didn't even know her—

Tina glanced up. Her brown eyes narrowed.

"Trent?" she called. "Is that you?"

Oops. "Uh . . . yeah," he answered uncertainly. He'd wanted a little more time to prepare—but now he had

to wing it. He felt a nervous flutter. Whatever. He could pull it off. There were basically two parts to Laurie's plan. The easy part was convincing Tina that he was too sad to get anything done because he and his girlfriend had just broken up.

The hard part was convincing Tina to skip school and go to LotsaFunland with him.

Still, he always worked best under pressure. It was just like playing the clutch quarter in a basketball game. He bowed his head and shuffled into the classroom, then slouched beside her.

"Hey," he mumbled, staring down at the desktop.

"Hey." Her eyes narrowed even more. "What's the matter? Are you all right?"

He laughed feebly. "Not really," he muttered.

"It's not anything serious, is it?" she asked.

"Well . . ." Forget the nervousness; this was a breeze. Her tone was so concerned. Not five seconds had passed, and she was already buying every false word that came out of his mouth. Amazing. Maybe he should be an actor. It wasn't any more difficult than putting on a Halloween costume. The only difference was that the disguise was invisible. "I . . . uh, I have to be honest with you," he said. "I didn't do my homework. Not such a great job for the second day of summer school, is it?"

"Not really," she answered, frowning. "But if you're not up for this today, I totally understand—"

"No, no. I'll be okay."

"Are you sure?"

He sighed and looked her straight in the eye. "Well, 'sure' might be pushing it. Do you know who Laurie Penrow is?"

Tina nodded, swallowing. Her brow was tightly knit. "Yeah. She's your girlfriend, right?"

He shook his head. "Not anymore."

"What?" she whispered. "What happened—" She broke off in midsentence. "Oh, I—I—I'm sorry," she stammered. "It's none of my business—"

"No, it's fine. To tell the truth, it would probably do me some good to talk about it."

Tina didn't say anything. She simply stared at him, waiting. And he could tell by her expression that she was excited now—and that she didn't want him to know it. Her big eyes were very bright and attentive. Wow. Maybe Laurie *was* right. Maybe Tina *did* like him.

"I don't really know what happened," he went on. "I mean, I guess it was kind of mutual. We both want different things. Like, she's into her whole social scene. Which is cool. But I . . . I . . ." He didn't finish. Instead he hauled his book bag up onto his desk and unzipped

it with a quick, jerky motion—pretending to be on the verge of losing control. "Forget it. Let's just talk about Shakespeare. You said this play is supposed to be funny, right? I could use a good laugh right now—"

"Listen, Trent, why don't you take the day off?" Tina interrupted. "I can tell Mrs. Witherspoon and Mr. Logan that you're sick or something. . . ."

Day off? He fought the urge to smile. Laurie was a genius. The plan was coming together now—a lot more quickly than he'd expected, too. The zipper slipped from his grasp. His shoulders slumped. "Well, to be honest, there *are* places I'd rather be than here," he said.

Tina nodded soberly. "I understand. Go on. I'll tell her. Just go home."

He glanced out the windows of the stuffy classroom onto the front lawn. "The thing is, I *can't* really go home," he said under his breath. "My dad's working at home today. He'd kill me if he found out I skipped summer school. I'm in enough trouble already."

"Well, there has to be somewhere you can go to take your mind off things," Tina insisted. "I mean, you could just go for a drive or something. It's such a beautiful day."

His gaze shifted back to her. "You know, you're right. It *is* a beautiful day. And I know just the place to go to take my mind off things." His face brightened—but he made sure to maintain a trace of sadness, just to keep the act convincing. "LotsaFunland."

Tina laughed. "I guess that would do it," she said. "That's a good idea. Go to LotsaFunland, ride on the Ferris wheel, eat corn dogs—"

"Why don't you come with me?"

She blinked. "What?"

"Tell Mrs. Witherspoon that something came up. Tell her I never showed and you have to go home."

Her jaw dropped. "Bu-But I—I . . . ," she stammered. "I don't think I could—"

"Why not?" he interrupted. "This way we can both have a good time and I can still learn about Shakespeare. You can tell me all about *The Taming of the Shrew* while we're on the Jupiter Bounce, about to puke our guts out."

Tina laughed again. Trent couldn't help but notice she was blushing slightly. "Jeez, when you put it that way . . ."

"Good," he said. "Then it's settled."

LotsaFunland Amusement Park—"The pride of North Conroe" as everyone jokingly referred to it—was nothing more than a motley collection of twenty out-of-date rides

and a Ferris wheel, stuck in the dust in the middle of nowhere off Route 40. In a town where the most exciting places to hang out were parking lots (the ones behind McDonald's and the multiplex theater being particular favorites), LotsaFunland was by far the hippest, wildest, coolest place a kid could go. But it was best not to think about those sorts of things. Military school might almost seem appealing if Trent really stopped to consider how deathly boring life could get around here.

"Hey, Tina, are you sure you're cool with this?" he asked.

"Huh?" She smiled quickly at him, then turned back to the road. She hadn't said one word in about fifteen minutes. "Oh yeah. I'm fine."

He stole a quick glance at her as they raced down the highway in his father's Jeep. She looked a little anxious. She sat rigid, drumming the fingers of her right hand on the armrest. *Jeez,* he thought. Either she liked him a lot—or she felt extremely guilty about lying to Mrs. Witherspoon and cutting work. But now that he thought about it, the latter was probably closer to the truth. It was only her second day on the job, after all.

Tina caught Trent looking at her and flashed him a shy grin. Her cheeks were flushed, bringing out her dark eyes. She really wasn't bad looking. Really a little cute. And funny in a goofy kind of way.

Trent smiled to himself. Laurie was wrong about Tina. Under other circumstances, the three of them might have been friends.

"You know, I've never been in a car with a car phone," she remarked.

Trent shrugged, glancing down at the little cellular next to the gearshift. "I don't even know if it works," he said. "We hardly ever use it."

She nodded distractedly. "So . . . are you feeling any better yet?"

"A little, I guess." He sighed, turning his attention back to the road. There was hardly any traffic. Heat rose from the asphalt and the flat desert in ripples. It must have been close to a hundred degrees today—and not a cloud in sight. Perfect for LotsaFunland. "It's just . . . I was thinking that this sort of feels like déjà vu. Laurie and I used to come out here together."

Tina nodded. "I know what you mean," she said in a faraway voice.

Trent glanced at her again. "You do?"

"Yeah." She laughed sadly. "I was thinking the same thing. The last time I went to LotsaFunland, I was with Laurie."

"What?" Trent almost slammed on the brakes. He gaped at her for a few seconds before remembering that

he was supposed to be driving a car. "When did you . . ."

"It was in the fifth grade," Tina said casually. "Back then, Laurie and I were pretty good friends. I bet you didn't know that, huh?"

No. I sure didn't.

His mouth hung open. He stared blankly at the pavement as it rushed under his wheels. Was this *true?* It couldn't be. Still . . . Tina didn't exactly strike him as a liar. In fact, now that he thought about it, Laurie *was* a little overly obsessed with Tina—considering that Tina was a complete stranger and not even part of their crowd.

But why would Laurie lie to him?

"I wouldn't be surprised if she never mentioned it," Tina said in the silence, as if reading his mind. "I'm sure she's embarrassed that she ever associated with someone like me."

Probably, Trent thought, but he didn't say anything. His grip tightened on the wheel. This was *not* part of the plan. Laurie hadn't told him anything about being friends with Tina. In a way, she'd lied to him. Here he was, following Laurie's instructions to trick Tina into going to LotsaFunland with him—but *he* was just a pawn in Laurie's plan, too.

Was that fair? No. Not at all. In fact, he was pretty

ticked off. He hadn't really wanted any part of this in the first place. It was *mean*. And now *he* was being manipulated. In a way, he was like a marionette, dancing on Laurie's strings. After all, she was the only one who knew the whole truth. He remembered how all the guys on the basketball team had made fun of him when he'd first started going out with Laurie—guys like Josh Frederick, who'd said: "Watch it, man. That chick's gonna have you on her leash." Trent figured he just was envious. Who wouldn't be? Laurie was the ultimate catch. But maybe, crazily enough, Josh was looking out for him. There was no denying certain facts—the longer Trent went out with Laurie, the more he catered to her every whim. . . .

". . . didn't mean to bring this stuff up," Tina was saying.

"What?" Trent blinked. "No, really. It's okay."

"Maybe we shouldn't talk about Laurie," Tina murmured.

Trent shook his head. He was going to find out all he could about Laurie's past relationship with Tina. "I don't mind," he said. "I'm actually kind of curious. Were you guys good friends?"

"Yeah, actually, we were."

"What happened? Why did it end?"

Tina sighed and stared out the window. "We kind of had a falling-out."

He blinked at her. "What do you mean?"

"It started on my eleventh birthday. We spent all of our birthdays together when we were little—I mean, ever since I could remember. So, that summer between fifth and sixth grade we had big plans for a birthday party for me, and she blew me off. . . . I don't know. The whole thing was so stupid. We got through the summer, but by the time we started middle grade, it was pretty clear she didn't want to be friends with me anymore. It was like I embarrassed her in front of her new friends or something." Tina glanced over at him and gave a dry little laugh. "You know what she told me once? 'My mom says you're not of our element.' Those were her exact words. 'Not of our element.'" Tina laughed bitterly. "Can you believe that?"

Actually, I can, Trent thought grimly. Mrs. Penrow's picture should have been printed in Webster's dictionary next to the word *snob*.

But there had to be something more to the story than Tina was revealing. If Laurie had dumped Tina as a friend five years ago, why would Laurie harbor any ill feelings now? Why would she even *care* about Tina? Maybe Tina had done something to her. Something in revenge. Or maybe this was Tina's revenge—trying to steal Laurie's boyfriend now, five years later. That was the only reasonable explanation. Or was it? This whole thing wasn't making any sense. And Trent really didn't like the idea that this perfect stranger could so easily make him doubt his own girlfriend.

"I'm sorry, Trent," Tina said, reading the look on his face. "I don't mean to be so harsh about your ex-girlfriend. This is all ancient history—totally forgotten."

He shook his head. "Don't worry about it," he muttered. But his brain was stewing in a dozen uncertain and troubling emotions. It was so . . . *confusing*. He needed to be alone, to sort this all out.

"Are you sure you want to go to LotsaFunland?" Tina asked. "I mean, if it's going to bring back a lot of painful memories, we can—"

"No, I'm sure," he interrupted, a little too emphatically. He cast another quick sidelong glance at her. She didn't seem suspicious. Of course she didn't. How could she possibly know that this whole trip was an elaborate setup? That Laurie was on to her—one step ahead of her, in fact.

He felt an urge to turn the car around and go back to school. But Laurie would be furious. She hated when plans backfired, especially her own. He absently tapped the steering wheel. Laurie must have had a good reason to lie to him about this. She *loved* him. She must have been trying to spare his feelings in some way. He had no idea how . . . but it didn't matter. He couldn't let her down. No. He'd promised he'd do anything for her. He had no choice, in a way—because as she pointed out, she'd saved his butt from Stonybrook. Besides, he was almost there. He could already see the tip of the Ferris wheel, just over the crest of a small hill. He would just have to be patient and wait for an explanation.

"I'm actually kind of psyched to check it out after all this time," Tina said.

"Check what out?" Trent asked.

She laughed. "Hello? LotsaFunland. That's where we're going, remember? That big amusement park up on the right?"

Trent forced a smile. "Oh, right," he said. He tried to slip back into his invisible costume. It didn't seem to fit as well anymore. He swallowed. Tina might not suspect that anything was wrong yet, but she wasn't a fool. No matter what Laurie thought of her.

Tina

"So what do you feel like riding first?" Trent asked.

Tina shrugged. "I dunno," she said. "You decide." After wandering around LotsaFunland for only ten minutes, she was starting to feel like she wasn't really living her own life—that instead she had been transported into some kind of bizarre alternate universe. Last week she had been staring at Trent from afar, daydreaming about saying hello. Yesterday she'd convinced herself that she was over him. Today she was strolling side by side with him, playing hooky from summer school.

It had all happened so fast. *Too* fast. How many romantic movies featured a scene in an amusement park: that pivotal scene where the boy always falls in love with the girl? At least a hundred. Probably more—

Hold on. She stopped herself. First of all, she *was* over that silly crush. Second of all (and most important), it was

chapter 8

very clear that he *wasn't* falling in love with her. Obviously he still had feelings for Laurie. Besides, if this were a movie, the amusement park would be a lot nicer than LotsaFunland. Everything here was just so . . . cheap. All the paint was peeling. The rides creaked and whined. None of the games had changed at all in five years. Even the prizes hadn't changed. If you shot the target with the little plastic rifle at the Bang-o-rama, you still went home with a big stuffed Alf. Who *was* Alf, anyway?

"How about the Ferris wheel?" Trent suggested.

"Um . . ." Tina swallowed.

All at once she felt like a complete imbecile. She couldn't go on any of these rides. They cost money, and she didn't have any. Not one single penny. She hadn't brought any cash to school because she'd never imagined she'd end up *here*. Not that she would have had any cash to bring, anyway.

"What's the matter?" he asked.

She smiled weakly as her hand brushed over the front pocket of her jean shorts, where her empty wallet was stuffed. "Well, I was planning on a nice quiet day reading Shakespeare, and here I find myself in the middle of LotsaFunland . . . without the cash to support my new Ferris wheel habit. I—I didn't bring any money—" she stammered, avoiding his eyes.

"Don't sweat it," he interrupted good-naturedly. "This is my treat."

Tina instantly shook her head in protest.

"I insist." He grinned. "Hey, look, *I'm* the one who convinced you to skip work today. It's the least I can do."

"I don't know. . . ." This was a serious dilemma. She stared down at their footprints in the dust. Maybe she should just take him up on his offer. After all, the situation couldn't get any more awkward, could it? And it was clear he wanted to stay. She shouldn't let her own pride get in the way of his good time. But the thought of his paying for her made her cringe.

Laurie used to pay for her, too. At the time, Tina had assumed it was just the gesture of a friend who cared about her. But later, after their friendship had ended, she worried that maybe that wasn't it at all. Maybe it was charity. And Tina didn't want charity from anyone.

She shook her head. Trent was right—coming back here was like déjà vu. Part of Tina felt like she was eleven years old again. The smell of popcorn and corn dogs, the dust in the hot air, the delighted shrieks of little kids . . . it was a sensory overload that unleashed a flood of powerful memories—and most of them were of Laurie.

There was no denying that Tina and Laurie had shared a lot of laughs at this dump. Like that time they

snuck into The Wacky Shack! and broke it. The Wacky Shack! was probably the *least* wacky place on earth: a tiny metal room that looked like a prison cell and rocked back and forth about as powerfully as a rowboat on a millpond. Needless to say, Tina and Laurie wanted to make it a little more exciting, just to get their money's worth. So they decided to jump up and down in it as hard as they could . . .

"What's so funny?" Trent asked.

"Huh?" Tina stopped short. She hadn't even realized she'd been laughing to herself. Her face reddened. "Nothing. It's just that, um, I was just thinking how the name LotsaFunland is a little misleading."

Suddenly he looked concerned. "What do you mean? Do you want to go home? I really don't mind treating you—"

"No, no." She shook her head. "I was just thinking that this place should be called, like, 'Pretty-Fun Land' or 'A Little Better Than Dull Land but Not Much.'"

Trent smiled. "Yeah, I know exactly what you mean. At the very least they shouldn't call it LotsaFunland *Amusement* Park. LotsaFunland *Boredom* Park would be a lot more . . . more . . ." He snapped his fingers.

"Appropriate?"

He beamed at her. "Yeah. That's exactly what I was

going to say. See, what did I tell you? I *knew* that coming here would be an educational experience." He started laughing.

Tina quickly turned away, gazing up the dirt path toward the huge Ferris wheel. She had to try not to stare at him. The problem was that when he laughed, his smile went crooked, and these little crinkly lines formed by his blue eyes—and for an instant he looked really goofy. And cute. And very sweet. But so what? She took a deep breath. She did *not* have a crush on him anymore. Period. They were just two people hanging out—nothing more than that.

"We could always just keep wandering aimlessly," Trent joked.

Tina nodded, breathing a secret sigh of relief. She smiled up at him. Their gazes locked. She expected him to look away. He didn't. He stared right back at her. Her heart skipped a beat. There seemed to be something different in his face, but she couldn't put her finger on it. It was as if he were looking at her for the first time. His eyes had a new intensity. But they seemed troubled as well. She held her breath. Was there something he wanted to tell her?

"You know, I bet we could go on the Ferris wheel for free," he stated in the silence.

That's not what you wanted to say, was it? Tina wondered, but she kept her mouth shut.

"Yeah," he continued. For once his voice sounded clumsy. "See, my buddy Josh Frederick is in charge of it, and—" He abruptly stopped. His eyes widened. He started shaking his head. His lips trembled.

"What's wrong?" Tina asked.

"I don't believe it," he croaked.

"What?" She turned and followed the direction of his gaze.

Laurie?

Tina's stomach lurched. She blinked, just to make sure she wasn't hallucinating. But that was Laurie, all right. That mane of blond curls was unmistakable. She was standing on the dirt path, decked out in a fashionable sundress, not twenty yards away.

"Oh, man." Trent groaned. He began shifting on his feet. "This is not good. . . ."

A realization struck Tina at that moment: Confessing to Trent that she was broke was *not* the most awkward set of circumstances that could arise. Nope. She felt like she'd just plummeted from the peak of a roller coaster. The sensation in her gut was about a thousand times more nauseating than any ride at LotsaFunland.

Laurie was staring at them now. She stepped forward. Her eyes narrowed.

Let's run the other way, Tina silently pleaded. *Let's run away—*

"Oh, *man*," Trent whispered out of the corner of his mouth. "Just what I didn't need."

Tina's eyes darted to Laurie. *Oh no.* She was walking toward them, looking very confused. *No, no, no.* This clandestine foray with Trent to LotsaFunland really *was* too perfect. She should have known better. Dreams didn't come true in real life. Of course not. Real life always went horribly wrong. She couldn't even flee. Her limbs seemed to have turned to jelly. She was petrified. And suddenly Laurie was right there . . .

"Hi," Laurie said tentatively, pushing her sunglasses up off her face and into her blond curls.

Tina didn't answer. Neither did Trent. He looked terrible, as if he'd seen a ghost.

Laurie's eyes flashed between the two of them. She didn't look confused anymore. In fact, her face was utterly expressionless—which was far more terrifying. "Um, shouldn't you be in summer school right now, Trent?" she asked.

Trent swallowed audibly and shrugged. "I guess."

"So what are you doing here?"

"You know . . . I really . . . I don't know," he said slowly. He took a step back. "You know, I think—uh, actually, I was just leaving."

Leaving? Tina frowned. They had just gotten there.

Without warning, Trent whirled and took off toward the parking lot. He was trucking so fast, he left a trail of dust flying behind him. Tina's mouth fell open. What was he *doing?* For a moment she was too stunned even to react. But by the time he disappeared around the corner of The Wacky Shack! she'd recovered enough to yell after him.

"Trent, wait!"

She shot a quick glance at Laurie. At least *she* looked flabbergasted, too. Tina couldn't believe this. Trent had dragged her all the way out here . . . and now he'd ditched her. Unbelievable.

"What's his problem?" Laurie murmured, as if to herself.

That was a very good question. And Tina was going to find out the answer. She scowled and drew in a deep breath, then ran after him—following the footprints, threading her way through the sparse crowd, nearly slamming into the Pitch-'n'-Putt booth, and finally emerging at the front gate: lungs heaving, face flushed, gasping for air . . . just in time to see Trent's Jeep peeling out of the parking lot.

"No," she choked out, horrified. "No!"

But it was too late.

The black vehicle disappeared into the sparse traffic on Route 40.

She shook her head. This couldn't be happening. She was stranded. He'd actually *stranded* her, knowing that she was flat broke. At LotsaFunland. With Laurie Penrow. Well. The day wasn't quite turning out to be *Romeo & Juliet*, was it? No. It was a little more along the lines of, say, *Scream*—or maybe *Halloween Part VII: The Revenge of Trent Rostand*.

Ha, ha, ha.

A lump started forming in Tina's throat. She blinked a few times. She was *not* going to cry. No. She would simply deal with the situation. She would find a phone and make a collect call to her mom at work and explain to her what had happened, and her mom would come and pick her up—

Somebody tapped her shoulder.

Tina spun around. *Laurie*. This was just great. Yup. Perfect. She gulped painfully, fighting back tears.

"Are you all right?" Laurie asked.

As if you care, Tina thought. But she kept her mouth shut.

Laurie peered at her closely. "What's going on?"

"Beats me," Tina muttered. She sniffed, struggling to regain enough composure to look Laurie in the eye. For the first time all day she felt the full brunt of the stifling Texas heat. Her knees wobbled. "Trent just took off. And I'm sort of stranded."

"Yeah, but . . . what are you two even doing here in the first place? I mean, aren't you supposed to be teaching Trent about Shakespeare or something right now?"

Tina glanced at her, bewildered. "How do *you* know about that?"

Laurie shrugged, gazing out at the parking lot. "He told me last night. He was raving about how he had the most awesome tutor—this girl named Tina Vasquez—and how he was going to have such a great time at summer school and blah, blah, blah." Her face soured. "It wasn't the most enjoyable conversation, as you might imagine."

In spite of her misery Tina felt a brief flicker of excitement. Trent had actually mentioned her? To *Laurie*, no less? But clearly he didn't care for Tina *that* much, or he wouldn't have run away like a jerk. Besides, there was a good chance he'd just said those nice things about his "awesome tutor" to make Laurie mad—*after* she'd dumped him.

"So do you need a ride back home?" Laurie asked.

"What?" Tina was sure she hadn't heard her correctly. Laurie Penrow couldn't be offering to do her a favor. It had never happened before—and it *certainly* wouldn't happen now.

Laurie raised her eyebrows. "You just said that you're stranded. I assume Trent gave you a ride, right?"

Tina didn't answer. She had no desire to relive the humiliation again.

"Look, I don't mind," Laurie said. "I know *you* didn't drive. I mean, I doubt you have your driver's license yet because your birthday isn't until July twenty-fourth."

Tina stared at her. *I can't believe you remember that.* But then . . . there was a reason the date would be stuck in Laurie's mind. Tina's eleventh birthday also happened to be the day that pretty much ended their long friendship.

An uneasy sensation tugged at Tina's insides. She knew that their falling-out wasn't entirely Laurie's fault. Tina had acted like a jerk, too. She'd stormed over to the Penrows' and basically thrown a tantrum in front of Laurie and her mother because Laurie had blown her off. Why did childhood traumas always feel so dramatic and important? To this day, Tina felt bad and embarrassed about what she'd done—but she'd been honest with Laurie, and she didn't have any regrets about *that*.

It had taken her a long time to move on and find new friends. She knew that she was better off for doing so, but part of her had always missed Laurie. She couldn't deny it.

Could it be that Laurie had deliberately mentioned her birthday as a kind of prelude to making peace? Maybe Laurie felt bad, too. Maybe being back at LotsaFunland conjured up the same kind of melancholy nostalgia in her as it did in Tina. It seemed unlikely that *any* emotion could exist inside that icy heart. But still . . .

Laurie offered a tentative grin.

"Look, I can understand if you wanted to get in a quick trip to The Wacky Shack! or something. But if you want a ride now, I'm going."

Much to her surprise, Tina found herself grinning, too. "It's funny you should mention The Wacky Shack!" she mumbled. "I was just thinking about our little fiasco, too."

"It's amazing we never got in trouble for that," Laurie said, glancing back at the park.

"We almost did," Tina pointed out.

"Luckily we could run fast."

"Also your mom screamed at the guy who was chasing us."

"'My daughter and her friend would have *nothing* to do with vandalism!'" Laurie quoted, in a dead-on impersonation of her mother's snooty voice.

Tina laughed. But then she stopped—as if she'd caught herself in a forbidden act. The day's dreamlike quality was quickly growing stranger, more surreal. Here she was with Laurie Penrow. A girl she wasn't supposed to like. Yet right now they were joking about the past like a couple of old buddies—and Laurie was clearly making an effort to be nice, to help Tina out of a jam. Why? Did Laurie feel guilty? Maybe in the aftermath of her breakup with Trent, she was just desperate to talk to somebody—*anybody* . . . even an ex-friend.

"Come on," Laurie insisted. "Let's get out of here."

Well, there was only one way to answer these questions. She could take Laurie up on her offer. Worst-case scenario: Laurie left her on the side of the road and drove off without her, too. But no matter what happened, her day really couldn't get much worse.

Laurie

chapter 9

Operation Sweet Sixteen was unfolding perfectly.

Laurie felt great. The top on her new convertible was down, and the hot summer wind was whipping through her curls. Even better, Trent had followed all of her instructions. She had to hand it to him—he was a superb actor.

Best of all, Tina was in the palm of her hand.

It was amazing how fast Laurie had gained Tina's trust. Of course, making fun of Mom had been a shrewd maneuver.

"Thanks so much for the ride," Tina said.

"No problem," Laurie replied. Her eyes were on the road, but she secretly watched Tina. The girl was checking out every square inch of the convertible's interior—staring at the CD player and mahogany dashboard, the tan leather seats. Her eyes were practically popping out of her head. *Please.* As if she'd never seen a BMW before.

What really bothered Laurie was that on closer inspection, she couldn't help noticing that Tina had turned into quite a looker while no one was watching. A natural beauty. It was still obvious that she didn't know how to dress, and she was in desperate need of a grown-up haircut, but the girl was gorgeous. Model material. And she was going to be sitting with Trent. Alone. Every day. For the whole summer . . .

"No, I mean it, really, thanks so much," Tina said again. "It's really nice of you. Especially after, you know . . ."

Laurie allowed herself a little smile. *Yeah, I know,* she answered silently. The infamous birthday incident and everything that came after it. The whole point of Operation Sweet Sixteen.

This payback had been a long time coming. Five whole years. The memory of that summer was still etched in Laurie's mind, as clearly as if it had happened last week. Just because Tina had turned eleven, Laurie was supposed to throw a ticker-tape parade? If only Tina understood the *embarrassment* she had caused. She had showed up on Laurie's doorstep (how did she even *get* there, anyway?), ranting and raving like a lunatic, blaming Laurie for all the problems in her life . . . when Laurie simply didn't want to be her friend anymore.

And it had nothing to do with where Tina lived, or the fact that she didn't have a pool, or any of that. No. Certain people just didn't mix. It was that simple.

The infuriating part of the whole thing was that Mom *still* mentioned it whenever she was disappointed in Laurie. Obviously Mom had been right about Tina all along. Obviously it was a good thing Laurie had dealt with Tina *then* instead of *now*. But even so . . . the ghost of Tina Vasquez still lurked around the Penrow household, ready to leap out and remind everyone of Laurie's past mistakes.

And the ghost of their friendship lingered at school, too—oh, not everyone remembered that golden girl Laurie Penrow had once been bosom buddies with Tina Vasquez, the girl from the other side of the tracks. But enough people remembered. And a few of them still brought it up. When Tina and her nerdy friends started that dumb literary magazine last year, Laurie's past came back to embarrass her once again. Her friend Carol had commented, "Aren't you friends with those dorks? I thought I remembered you hanging out with that Tina girl. . . ." As if that wasn't bad enough, Carol had said it in front of Trent and a few other kids. Laurie was horrified. She had set Carol straight, but how many other people still remembered the days when she and Tina were friends?

She had to make it very clear to everyone that Tina was ancient history—that as far as Laurie was concerned, their friendship had never happened.

If only Laurie could have made Tina understand how embarrassing it was for her—how being friends with a loser had almost ruined her chances at having any social life at all. Tina used to cry every day in sixth grade when Laurie and her new friends excluded her and ignored her. She followed Laurie around school and called her house every night, begging her to forgive her for whatever she'd done. Did she have any idea how humiliating that had been for Laurie? How bad it made her look? No, of course not.

She would, though. Very soon.

"This is a really great car," Tina remarked.

Laurie shrugged. "Thanks." *Here it comes,* she thought. Now Tina would start laying on the sob story about how she would *never* receive a birthday present like this. Yes. That was how Tina operated. She was subtle that way. By talking about herself and her problems, she would make *you* feel terrible. She might pretend to be grateful; she might even *feel* a little genuine gratitude toward Laurie for "rescuing" her . . . but there was no doubt in Laurie's mind that Tina would attempt to use this opportunity to her advantage. She would try to make Laurie feel guilty. She would try to pump Laurie for information about Trent.

Wasn't that Tina's own secret plan? To embarrass Laurie again. To steal her boyfriend. To take everything she had worked so hard for? Well, it wasn't going to happen. Laurie knew just how people like Tina operated. And she was way ahead of her former friend.

"So what were you doing out at LotsaFunland, anyway?" Tina's question broke into Laurie's thoughts and caught her off guard.

She squirmed in her seat. She hadn't even thought of an excuse. "I . . . uh, I don't know. I thought it would take my mind off things. It's been a rough twenty-four hours."

"Yeah, that's exactly what Trent said. I guess it's kind of natural that you two wound up at the same place."

Laurie shot her a quick glance. "What do you mean?"

"Um . . . you know, since you guys used to go there . . . you know, while you were going out," Tina mumbled incoherently. "I don't really know. It's none of my business. I'm sorry."

"No, it's all right," Laurie said. "I mean, obviously it is your business, right? Trent asked *you* to go there, didn't he?"

Tina didn't say anything. She blinked several times.

"Look, it's okay if he did," Laurie said. "I won't get mad or anything—"

"Well, he didn't do his homework," Tina interrupted. "So we figured there was no point in sticking around the classroom." The words tumbled out of Tina's mouth in a rush. "He seemed so depressed. I told him to go home. But he really wanted to go to LotsaFunland. I thought it would cheer him up. He asked me to go with him because he wanted to talk about *The Taming of the Shrew* while we were going on the different rides and stuff...." She started blushing.

Laurie feigned a look of concern. "What is it?"

"I just realized how incredibly ridiculous that sounds," Tina muttered. "But it's true. I swear, Laurie."

"I believe you," Laurie said casually. Of course she did. Tina was basically recounting Laurie's plan, word for word. She shifted lanes to pass a truck and stepped on the gas a little bit. The wind was roaring now. She raised her voice to be heard. "If you want to know the truth, the only reason I'm upset is because I showed up and ruined your day."

"What?"

Laurie sighed and forced a sad smile. This was the trickiest part: the lie on which the whole scheme depended.

She kept her eyes on the highway. "Can you keep a secret, Tina?"

"Uh . . . yeah, I guess," Tina said. Now she *really* looked uncomfortable.

"Last night when Trent was raving about what a great tutor you are, all I could think was: You and he would actually make a pretty good couple."

"What?" Tina cried.

Laurie nodded. "I know how that sounds. But it's true. Trent and I aren't really meant to be together. I knew that a long time ago. But for some reason, I could never bring myself to end our relationship. It's not that I don't like him. . . ." She swallowed, pretending to wrestle with her thoughts. "In a way, I *love* him—but as a friend. And I know that deep down, he probably realizes that *he* feels the same way about *me*. It's just tough to admit you're wrong about somebody. You know?"

Tina didn't answer. She was frozen stiff. Judging from the look on her face, you would think she'd been slapped or something.

"See, Tina, the kind of person Trent *really* needs is someone like you," Laurie said.

"You've got to be kidding me," Tina croaked.

Laurie laughed softly. "Maybe I'm wrong. But if

you're the same person you were when I knew you, then I'm right."

Tina kept quiet.

"Who knows?" Laurie said softly. "You could have changed a lot in the past five years. I can't really claim to know you anymore—"

"That was your decision, Laurie," Tina interrupted. "Not mine."

"Look, Tina . . . I know that a lot of what happened between us was my fault," Laurie lied. "But you have to understand. I was going through a tough time, trying to make new friends in a new school. And you know my family doesn't see things the way other people do. To them everything's black-and-white. In their eyes—especially my mother's—there are only two kinds of people: the kind you can associate with and the kind you can't."

"Thanks," Tina muttered sarcastically. "That makes me feel much better."

Laurie glanced at her again. Their eyes met for a moment.

"I'm sorry, Tina," she stated. "I really am." Her voice was steady. Resolute. She didn't even blink. Now, *that* was convincing. "I don't blame you for being angry with me. But I want you to know . . ." She bit her lip and turned back to the highway. "I want you to know that

I've been thinking about a lot of things lately. Most of them have to do with Trent, obviously—but a lot of them have to do with bad choices I've made. You know, things I've done because I felt like I had to please other people."

Again Tina kept quiet. But her face seemed to soften a little.

"I guess what I'm really trying to say is that in spite of how it looks, this might be the best possible time to break up with Trent," Laurie added. She laughed ruefully. "Although *he* probably doesn't see it that way."

"Judging from the way he hightailed it out of there, I'd say not," Tina said.

Laurie's excitement rose. Yes, Tina's tone had changed. She no longer sounded puzzled or upset. Laurie's little speech had affected her. Definitely. She was letting down her guard.

It was time to move in for the kill.

"Look, I know I'm not in a position to ask you any favors or anything like that," Laurie said. "But do you think that maybe you could go easy on him in class for a little while? You know—just help him out a little?"

Tina exhaled deeply. "I guess," she mumbled. "I don't really know what I could do, though. To be honest, I don't even really know how to tutor."

"I'm sure you'll come up with something," Laurie said. "Just think of it as a way of paying me back for giving you a ride home."

"Talk about extortion," Tina joked.

Laurie cocked an eyebrow. "Well, you know me."

The two of them laughed together. It was so easy, so natural. Just like old times. And that was the beauty of it. With a couple of well-phrased lies, Laurie had shoved Tina right into position for the prank of a lifetime.

You're mine, Tina. I'll put you in a place where you won't ever be able to embarrass me again.

Something was terribly wrong.

Laurie knew it the moment she arrived home. Trent's Jeep was already parked in the Penrows' vast driveway—but he was standing in front of the garage door, arms folded across his chest, his jaw squarely set. *Uh-oh.* Usually if Trent showed up at her house before she did, he simply went around back and hung out by the pool. If Laurie hadn't known better, she'd say that he almost looked . . . well, *angry*. But what on earth did he have to be angry about? The plan had gone off without a hitch. They had both turned in brilliant performances.

"We have to talk," he called as she slowed to a stop in front of him.

Laurie swallowed. She turned off the engine and shoved her keys into her purse.

"What's the matter?" she asked cautiously.

Trent marched over to the convertible and opened the driver's side door for her. "You lied to me," he stated, stepping aside. "*That's* what's the matter."

Tina, Laurie realized. Her blood ran cold. She sat there in the car, staring up at him. The sun beat down on her. She began to wilt. Of course. *Tina must have told Trent about how she was friends with me.*

She should have seen this coming. Trent had no idea of her past, and Laurie had worked very hard to keep it that way. Even her own mother advised her not to mention it. The wrong associations could taint a person's reputation for years. Laurie's association with Tina *had* tainted her reputation—before high school. That was why she'd lied to Trent about how she found the note; if he knew that she'd actually gone through the garbage looking for something Tina wrote, he might suspect that there was some history between them. He might suspect that the summer school scheme was less about him and more about Tina Vasquez.

And that wasn't true—not entirely. Laurie wanted Trent to ace English, to stay in North Conroe. That really was how the whole thing started. She found out

about Tina by accident. It was just lucky for her that she realized what Tina was up to—trying to steal her boyfriend right from under her nose, humiliate her. So she had a few ulterior motives; so what? This way everyone could get what they wanted: Trent could stay and be her boyfriend, and Tina, well, she'd be put in her place for good. Laurie would never have to worry about her again.

Stupid, she scolded herself. She should have been more open with Trent. Now he wouldn't trust her, and that could ruin everything. But the thing was, Trent would never understand her point of view. He would never understand why Tina deserved such harsh treatment. No. He was a *guy*. Guys just couldn't comprehend what went on between girls or even what was important to them.

"You want to tell me what happened?" she finally asked.

"Sure," he said. "I followed your instructions exactly. I convinced Tina to go to LotsaFunland. We 'accidentally' bumped into you. I took off, just like you told me—"

"I know, Trent, and you were so convincing—"

"Why don't you let me *finish,* all right? You told me that you 'wanted an opportunity to get to know Tina.'"

He made angry little quotation marks in the air with his fingers. "You said that awkward circumstances were the best time to make new friends because their defenses were down. You acted like you didn't know her at all. And then I find out you guys were, like, *best* friends. So what's going on, Laurie?"

Laurie slumped back in her seat. This was even worse than she'd imagined.

"I didn't mean to keep you in the dark," she said, stalling. "And I wasn't really lying. I mean, I *don't* know Tina. I haven't spoken to her in almost five years—"

"Oh, come off it." He groaned.

She sighed. She should have known that lame defense wouldn't work. "I just didn't think you'd understand where I was coming from," she admitted.

"Well, try me!" he cried. "I mean, I feel like I deserve an explanation, you know? I could have screwed everything up for you. I could have confronted you in front of Tina and asked what was going on." He took a deep breath and lowered his voice. "But I figured I owed you."

Now she felt *really* bad. Trent had kept his word, even though she had been dishonest. Well, she hadn't exactly lied. She just hadn't told the whole truth. And he *did* owe her . . .

"Why are you so mad at her? Did she do something to you?" Trent prompted.

"Sort of. It's complicated."

"How complicated can it be? Either she did something or she didn't."

Hmmm. On second thought, maybe she didn't feel so bad. He almost sounded like he was sticking up for Tina. What did he know about this? Nothing . . . unless Tina had told him about it from *her* self-serving perspective. But she probably left out the part about how Laurie's mom practically threatened to disown her if she kept hanging around with Tina Vasquez.

All right, that was an exaggeration. Still, it *was* hard for Laurie to make new friends after Tina—to prove to all the other girls that Tina hadn't corrupted her. Hanging out with that girl had cost her *years* of acceptance. It wasn't really until she'd gotten to high school and met new people that her life changed. In fact, it wasn't *really* until she started going out with Trent that her slate had been completely wiped clean. And now Tina wanted to take it all away from her. No way.

"I'll tell you what she did," Laurie said. "She made me feel like dirt. *Lower* than dirt. I was *always* a good friend to her. Always. But she made it seem like I *owed* her or something. And then when I finally had enough, she tried to ruin my life. You weren't there; you couldn't know." Laurie's lips pressed into a tight line. "Look, all you need to know is that Tina is extremely jealous of me—she's out to get me."

The memory of that horrible day, Tina's birthday, came back, and a jumble of disjointed sentences swirled through Laurie's mind... *How can you do this to me?... I thought you were my best friend.... You have no feelings.... What makes you think you're so special?* She could see the veins bulging in Tina's eleven-year-old neck, the wetness on her flushed cheeks. She shoved the memories aside. Enough. If a birthday party was what Tina Vasquez wanted, then that was what she would get.

Yes. She was going to get a party, all right. The party of a lifetime.

"Hey." Trent leaned over her. "You're really shook up. What happened between you two? Are you really that scared of her?"

"I'm not scared of her. The point is, Tina's going after *you* now," Laurie stated. "And it sounds like she actually got you to sympathize with her."

Trent reached out and gently laid a hand on her shoulder. "I'm sorry," he said. "I didn't know you two had a history."

Laurie shook her head. "It's all right. I should have

told you everything right from the start. It's just . . . I don't know."

"Don't worry about it," he said. "I understand."

"So are you still with me?" Laurie asked, gazing up into his eyes.

He looked at her. "Laurie, I don't get this. I mean, if you've got a problem with Tina, I don't want to get in the middle. I'm starting to think that I should ask for another tutor. . . ."

"No!" Laurie yelled. She got out of the car and slammed the door hard. "Don't do this to me! I can't believe it—she always turns everyone against me. . . ." Laurie burst into tears.

Trent gathered her up in his arms. "Hey, it's okay. I'm not turning against you. I just don't think you're going to make things better with all this scheming. Why don't we just leave all of this in the past?"

"Because Tina won't leave it in the past. I have to put her in her place, once and for all, to stop her from ruining my life. And I need your help. Now, are you in or out?" Laurie's dark blue eyes were rimmed with tears.

Trent just stared at her, unable to answer.

"Remember, you owe me. I helped you when you needed me. . . ."

"You're right. I guess I'm in," Trent said. "But just what are you planning to do? And be honest with me this time."

"Nothing much. I'm just going to make up for how I ruined her eleventh birthday."

Trent blinked. His face was troubled. "How will you do that?"

She smiled and waved her hand at the house. "I'm going to throw a birthday bash for her. A Sweet Sixteen. Right here."

"But what about your parents?" he asked, frowning. "I thought they hated Tina—"

"They're not going to be here," Laurie interrupted. "They're going to L.A. for the last ten days in July. So I'll have the house to myself. And I'm going to throw the biggest blowout ever, something Tina would never be able to afford herself." Laurie raised her eyebrows. "And *you're* going to be the bait."

Trent

chapter 10

The next morning Trent found himself hesitating once again in the hall outside the tutoring classroom—only this time he was just as wide awake as Tina. And he should have been exhausted. He hadn't been able to get much sleep last night. Even though the air conditioner in his bedroom had been cranked, he'd felt hot and out of breath, as if the sheets were suffocating him.

The problem was, his *life* was suffocating him.

Okay. That was an overstatement. In theory, his life was better than ever. Laurie was happy. Her grand plans were coming together. So why did he feel so *trapped?* He could understand being cranky about having to play a charade with Tina—and yes, even still a little ticked off that Laurie had lied to him—but these were minor inconveniences compared to the big picture. Anyway, he'd correctly guessed Laurie's motives for hiding the truth in the first place: She didn't want him to feel sorry for her. Besides, judging from what she'd said, he guessed her feelings toward Tina were justified.

But she was still pulling the strings, wasn't she? Maybe he was just annoyed by her choice of words yesterday: *"And you're going to be the bait."* It was almost as if he weren't a real person. He *was* a puppet. And now he had to dance on into that classroom and put on another act just to keep Laurie's plan on track.

The worst part of all was that he couldn't argue with Laurie about any of this. She *had* kept him in school. And he knew how she could get when she became angry. If she'd kept him *out* of Stonybrook, she could just as easily find a way to put him back in.

He shook his head and peered through the cracked door window at Tina.

Her hair was in pigtails again. She was sitting there reading, just like yesterday, looking so *innocent*. But she wasn't. She had been cruel to his girlfriend. Right. He had to remember that. Besides, he liked acting, didn't he? Yes. He just needed to psych himself up for another performance. It was just like a basketball game. He didn't *always* want to play. But when it came time for him to hit the court—

"You're not thinking of running away again, are

you?" Tina called with a smile. She didn't take her eyes from the page.

Oh, brother. He would really have to stop loitering around the door like this. He took a deep breath, then sauntered in and sat beside her. He grinned apologetically. "Tina, look, I just wanted to say that I'm really sorry about bolting yesterday and—"

"Don't worry," she interrupted.

"But it was so lame of me...."

"Yes, that's true," she said, smirking. "But it's all right. I forgive you. Things managed to work out in a very weird way."

"How's that?" he asked, even though he already knew the entire story.

"Well, after you *ditched* me, Laurie gave me a ride back to school." She deliberately emphasized the word *ditched*—obviously to heap on the guilt. "Laurie Penrow actually did me a favor." Tina shook her head, as if she still didn't believe it. "We had a pretty normal conversation, too. Anyway, I understand why you freaked out and bolted. Don't worry. No hard feelings."

He sighed, pretending to be very relieved. Of course, Laurie had told him that Tina wouldn't be mad. He was already back in costume, performing again. Just like that. Without thinking. He had to say one thing for

Tina: She definitely put him at ease, which made Laurie's plan much easier. Today he was supposed to find out as much as he could about Tina's geeky personal life—in hopes of finding out some kind of embarrassing information they could exploit for the prank at the Sweet Sixteen.

Sure, Laurie was being just a *little* overzealous . . . but on the other hand, Trent had seen the pain in her face yesterday. He knew that Tina had hurt her something bad. "Well, I want to make it up to you," he said.

Tina flashed him a wry grin. "You can start by doing your homework. I don't suppose you read last night's assignment, did you?"

"Uh . . ."

"I figured," she said. She rolled her eyes good-naturedly. "What are we going to do with you, Trent? It's the third day of summer school, and somehow you already managed to get three days behind."

"I know, I know," he said. "It's just . . ."

"You're going through a rough time," she finished, but her tone was gentle.

He glanced down at her copy of *The Taming of the Shrew*. It looked so worn, with its cracked spine and frayed cover. His copy, on the other hand, still looked brand-new. He hadn't touched it once since he'd bought it.

"What's the matter?" she asked.

"I was just thinking how much I wish I could walk into Mr. Logan's class with *your* book instead of mine. He'll take one look at it and know I haven't read squat."

Tina laughed. "I'll tell you what. I'll lend you my copy. It has a bunch of notes in the margins, and all the important passages are already underlined. That way you won't be lost. Not totally, anyway."

His face brightened. "Really? Wow, that would be—"

"You still have to *read* it, though, Trent."

"Yeah, yeah . . . of course." He reached over and picked it up. Their gazes met. "Thanks a lot, Tina. That's really nice of you." And for the first time since this bizarre episode started, Trent realized that the words coming out of his mouth were sincere. Lending him the book *was* nice of Tina.

He realized something else at that moment, too: Telling the truth felt better than lying. Honesty worked. Even professional actors knew that. He'd seen interviews with famous Hollywood types; they were always rambling on about bringing "reality" to their characters. And this was no different. He resolved to tell the truth to Tina as much as possible without giving away Laurie's plan. At least he could look into Tina's eyes with absolute confidence during the few times he didn't have to lie.

"So . . . uh, it looks like we have another hour to kill, yet again," Tina said. "Any suggestions?"

"Want to go to LotsaFunland?" Trent joked.

Tina pursed her lips. "Very funny. You know, maybe I should just leave you alone with William Shakespeare this morning." She nodded at the book in his hands, then reached down to pick up her knapsack. "You can spend the hour doing schoolwork for a change—"

"No, no," he protested. And he really *didn't* want her to leave. "Wait. I mean . . . that's no fun. For either of us."

"Speak for yourself." She laughed. "I'm going outside to lie in the sun."

"But isn't that shirking your tutorial duty?" he asked, trying to sound dramatic.

She let go of her knapsack. "You know, Trent, I have to tell you something. I don't want to sound like a concerned parent or anything, but you're pretty smart for somebody who's getting Cs in English. I mean, your vocabulary is better than mine. I'm not just saying that, either."

"I *know!*" he cried. "I mean, not that my vocabulary is better than yours," he added quickly. "But, like, this is the root of all my problems." He couldn't help but smile. Honesty really *did* work. He was amazed at how content he felt. He was engaged in a simple dialogue with his tutor. No subtext.

"See, I *love* to read. But I think I must have that thing—you know, that thing that everyone's talking about these days . . . attention deficit disorder. Because every time I sit down with something like *this*"—he waved Tina's book in the air to drive home his point—"my brain shuts down. I just can't concentrate."

She laughed again.

"What?"

"It's not ADD, Trent. It's just that you probably get turned off by the language. I mean, when *I* was first assigned Shakespeare, I didn't know what the hell he was talking about, either. But once you get over that, it's like . . . this whole new world opens up. Seriously. And I know that sounds really cheesy, but it's true."

He nodded eagerly. This was important stuff. It didn't sound cheesy at all. If he could actually learn to *enjoy* Shakespeare, then he'd be set for life. "How did you get over it, or get used to it, or whatever?" he asked.

"I checked out some of his sonnets. They're nice and short, so they're a lot less intimidating than his plays. Once you start getting into the language . . ." Tina's voice trailed off.

"You really like poetry, huh?" Trent asked.

She grinned. "Hey. You're supposed to be reading right now. Not procrastinating."

"But this is important," he argued, even though he was grinning himself again, too. "Really. I mean, if I find out how somebody as smart and sharp and insightful as *you* got into poetry, then I can follow that example myself—"

"Flattery will *not* get you a good grade," she interrupted, but she was blushing.

He raised his hands. "Hey. I'm just telling the truth. So how *did* you get so into poetry, anyway?"

"I don't really know," she mumbled. "A couple of friends of mine who also write for *Deep Ellum* got me into it."

"Deep what?"

"*Deep Ellum*. North Conroe High's literary magazine? Home of the sharpest, smartest, and most insightful writers around? You *never* heard of it?" she teased.

"Uh . . . well . . ."

"I bet I can find a copy to show you. . . ." She sat up straight and craned her neck, glancing around the classroom. Her gaze zeroed in on a small bookshelf under the blackboard. "Yup. Bingo." She hopped out of the chair and strode to the front of the class, then removed what looked like a yearbook. "Prepare to be dazzled," she said dryly, handing the book to him. She sat down again.

Trent opened the leather-bound cover and began

flipping through the pages. He had no idea that North Conroe High published a literary magazine. It actually looked a lot cooler than he would have thought: There were photographs and drawings interspersed with the poetry and stories, almost like a magazine. Some of the drawings were pretty outrageous, too. He caught a glimpse of a couple of half-naked women, a guy who looked like a burnt-out rock star, smoking a cigarette. . . .

"Hey, there's your name!" he said.

Tina leaned over his shoulder, almost brushing his cheek with her silky hair. "Uh, yeah," she said dismissively. "That's just a stupid little haiku I wrote."

Trent found he was strangely distracted by being this close to her. Did he hear her correctly? "Uh, a what?"

"It's this Japanese form of poetry. You can only use seventeen syllables. Five on the first line, then seven, then five."

Trent peered at the page.

HAIKU FROM A SECRET ADMIRER
BY TINA VASQUEZ

> If you know I'm here,
> Please give me a sign: a glance.
> Or smile, if you can.

Wow, he thought. That was pretty cool. But maybe he just thought he liked it because it was so short. No . . . it had a mysterious, anonymous kind of vibe—and it appealed to him. It reminded him a little of song lyrics, only the words didn't rhyme.

"You know, that's really neat," he said. "It says a lot without having to say much at all. I mean, it's like, you can tell that the girl in the poem is totally in love with this guy, and she's hopeful, too. And you sort of get the feeling that she might have a chance, but the guy can't do anything. . . ." Suddenly he felt stupid. He had no idea what he was talking about. How could *he* know what she meant? He looked up. "Wait. This is a girl talking, right? I mean, I just assumed—" He stopped himself.

Tina's face had turned a fiery red.

"I'm sorry, am I totally embarrassing you?"

"Uh . . . no." She fumbled for her book bag. Her chair screeched on the floor. "It's, uh, I just remembered I have to call my mom." She jumped up and hurried out of the classroom, clumsily struggling to gather her unzipped book bag in her arms. "Go ahead and borrow my book. I'll see you later—"

The door slammed behind her.

"Hey, wait!" Trent called, baffled.

But Tina's muted footsteps were already clattering down the hall.

He frowned. Now, *that* was weird. One second they were discussing haikus; the next, she was bolting. Maybe *she* was playing a prank on *him*—trying to get him back for yesterday. Well, she'd succeeded. He couldn't help but feel a little gypped, too. She was his *tutor*, right? It was her job to stay with him and help him learn, especially since he was really starting to appreciate this poetry stuff. He felt like he'd cleared away some cobwebs and rediscovered a long-forgotten part of his brain: a part that desperately needed an oil change and tune-up. And Tina was the brain mechanic. Or something like that. (He wasn't the poet; *she* was.) His eyes fell back to the page.

Oh, jeez.

He slapped his forehead and groaned. Man. He could be thick sometimes, couldn't he?

The poem was about *him*.

Obviously. And by allowing him to read it, Tina had accidentally announced that she *had* been in love with him. At least at one time. No wonder she took off. He slumped back in his chair and laughed miserably. To make matters worse, he'd pretty much told her that she had a decent shot with him—by talking in the third person about the "guy" in the poem.

Of course, that was exactly what Laurie *wanted* him to do. . . .

His smile faded.

Why did he feel so terrible all of a sudden?

This was *supposed* to happen. Laurie's plan was working.

But it wasn't as if Tina were sneaking around behind Laurie's back. Yesterday Laurie had practically encouraged her to make a move on Trent. Besides, as far as Tina knew, he and Laurie were finished. And Tina's advances weren't exactly slimy or low. No . . . they could hardly be called "advances" at all. She had showed him a love poem. By accident. You couldn't get much more innocent than that. He might even think that it was romantic if he were the kind of cheeseball guy who wore black turtlenecks and drank coffee and read . . . well, Shakespeare. But it *was* undeniably flattering. Anyway, she was long over her crush now. She'd written this last year.

He shook his head. All right. This entire scheme of Laurie's had gone too far. It was time to put an end to it. Maybe Tina had done something terrible to Laurie in the past, but they were little *kids* then. People changed. From what he could tell, Tina had become a perfectly nice person, a perfectly beautiful person, actually, albeit a little nerdy. What awful things had she done lately? Nothing. Not even close. She'd lent Trent her book. She'd forgiven him for ditching her at LotsaFunland. And most incredible of all, she'd actually done her job as a tutor in just a few days: She'd gotten him interested in poetry. Now, how amazing was *that*? He'd even had a semi-intellectual conversation with her.

Maybe Laurie just needed to open her eyes to the kind of person Tina had become. Laurie was stubborn, but she could learn. Tina was only trying to help him out. And he could begin taking advantage of that help if Laurie would just forget this stupid prank. Somehow in the midst of all the deception and mind games, summer school had been forgotten. That was what started this whole business in the first place, right?

Yes. It was time to start fresh. No more role playing. No more lying.

He smiled, feeling very much as if the marionette strings had finally been cut.

Tina

chapter 11

"You're not gonna *believe* what happened this morning," Tina grumbled into the telephone.

"Let me guess," Susan said. "Trent Rostand convinced you to go back to LotsaFunland, only *this* time Laurie wasn't around when he left you there, so you had to hitchhike home with some crazed religious fanatics."

"Ha, ha, ha," Tina moaned. She rolled over in her small twin bed, lying flat on her back.

It was only noon, but already she felt completely wiped out. At least Wednesdays were short days; she didn't have to tutor any students in the afternoon. She stared at the ceiling and twirled the phone cord around her fingers. Maybe she should just stay here in her bedroom for the rest of her life, nestled among all her old childhood stuffed animals. Yup. She would never get off her mattress again. She'd become one of those people who gain a thousand pounds so that they can't even *move* and then spend all her time eating and getting filmed by TV shows like *Jerry Springer* and *The Guinness Book* . . .

"So?" Susan asked. "What happened?"

Tina took a deep breath. "Trent saw the poem I wrote in *Deep Ellum*," she said. "You know, the haiku."

There was silence on the other end.

"Hello?" Tina asked.

Susan burst out laughing. "How did *that* happen?"

Tina squeezed her eyes shut. The truth was almost too painful to admit. "I kind of showed it to him."

"*What?*" Susan cried. "Jeez, Tina, I gotta hand it to you. You really operate quickly—"

"I didn't *mean* to," Tina protested, but she was laughing now, too—mostly out of despair. She opened her eyes. "It just kind of happened. I mean, Trent was asking how I got into poetry, and I just . . . I just . . . I don't even know. For some reason, I got the idea to show him the book."

"Well, I'm sure he'll never forget it," Susan muttered. "Did he know the poem was about him? He *must* have. What did he say?"

"I don't know," Tina said.

"What do you mean, you don't know?"

Tina bit her lip. "I kind of freaked out. I got so

embarrassed, I just ran out. I haven't seen him since. I hid in the girls' room until the study period was over."

Susan started cracking up again.

"It's not *funny!*" Tina cried—even though she knew very well that it was, in a tragic way. "The thing that stinks the most about this is that my crush on him is over; I mean, now that I've gotten to know him and everything." But for some reason, she knew the words didn't sound very convincing.

"So what are you going to do?" Susan asked.

"I was thinking plastic surgery. Or maybe I'll just head to the Mexican border. If I left now, I could probably make it there by sunrise—"

"Seriously, Tina." Susan's laughter finally subsided. "Maybe you should call him. Think of a really good excuse. You know, that you forgot to take your medication or something—"

There was a beep. Another call was coming in on the Vasquezes' line. "Wait, hold on a sec," Tina said. She pressed the flash button on the receiver. "Hello?"

"Hi, Tina?"

She sat up straight. Her pulse picked up a beat. That voice. It sounded uncannily like . . .

"Laurie?" she whispered.

"Yeah. How's it going?"

For a moment Tina couldn't respond. She stared blankly into space. This was crazy. Laurie Penrow hadn't called this house in almost five years. *Uh-oh.* Maybe Trent told Laurie about the poem. Maybe Laurie was calling because she wanted Tina to back off her turf. But no, Laurie and Trent were finished. In fact, judging from what Laurie had told her in the car yesterday, Tina thought Laurie would be *happy* that Tina had showed Trent the haiku—

"Tina? Are you there?"

"Uh . . . y-yeah," she stammered. She blinked hard. "Wait, can you hold on? I'm on the other line."

"Do you want to call me back?" Laurie asked.

Tina shook her head. Listening to the sound of Laurie's voice, you'd think that they still spoke by phone every single day. "No, no. Just hold on. I'll only be a second." She pressed the flash button. "Susan?" she whispered.

"Yeah? Do you have to go?"

"It's *Laurie*," Tina hissed.

"Laurie Penrow?" Susan sounded as incredulous as Tina felt.

"Yeah." Tina's heart was racing now. She didn't even know why she was so nervous. Talking on the phone was a lot less of a big deal than being stuck in a two-seater convertible for thirty minutes. The hard part was already over. *The hard part of what, though?* she asked herself. Was she becoming friends with Laurie again?

"Look, I better go. I'll call you when—"

"What does she want?" Susan interrupted.

"I have no idea. That's what I'm going to find out."

"Well . . . all right," Susan agreed reluctantly. "Call me back as soon as you're done."

"I will. Bye." Tina pressed the flash button one last time. "Laurie?"

"Hey," Laurie answered. "Are you sure you can talk?"

"Yeah," Tina replied cautiously. She propped herself up against her pillows. "So, what's up? Thanks again for the ride, by the way."

"No problem," Laurie said.

Neither of them spoke for a moment. Tina's mouth was very dry.

"Look, Tina, there's something I've been wanting to tell you." Laurie took a deep breath. "I just wanted to say . . . you know . . . that I meant what I said in the car."

Tina's throat tightened. She blinked a few times. "Go on," she managed.

Laurie laughed awkwardly. "I, um—I'm really not too good at these kinds of things, as I'm sure you know," she said. "I just mean . . . I guess what I *really* mean is that I'm sorry I screwed up your eleventh birthday."

As much as Tina hated to admit it, she'd been waiting for five years to hear those exact words. A powerful warmth seemed to spread in waves throughout her body. She almost felt like crying. "Look, Laurie," she croaked. "That was so long ago—"

"I know, I know." Laurie's voice seemed to regain some of its self-possession. "I guess I just want to make it up to you."

"Uh . . . why?" Tina's own voice was trembling now. Laurie really *was* reevaluating her life. "You don't have to. I mean, I said some things that I shouldn't have, and in some ways I'm as much to blame as you are—"

"No, no, no," Laurie said. "That's not true. Anyway, it doesn't matter. There's something I feel like I have to do. Something to make up for *all* the birthdays I missed." She paused. "I want to throw you a Sweet Sixteen party. Here. At my house. July twenty-fourth."

Tina nearly gasped. "What?"

"You heard me. I want to throw you that birthday party I promised you five years ago." That was it. Tina couldn't control herself anymore. Her eyes welled with tears. A lone drop fell from her lashes. Laurie had finally remembered her birthday. And Sweet Sixteen was *way* more important than number eleven. In fact, Tina had been dreading July 24 for the very reason that

it *was* a milestone, that it was *supposed* to be special.

It was incredible. Nobody had ever thrown her a birthday party before. Well, except for her mom. But that didn't count. Going out for pizza and getting a birthday cupcake hardly counted as a "party." Of course, she knew her mom couldn't afford to throw her a huge bash. Or even a small bash. The Vasquezes' little two-bedroom bungalow couldn't accommodate more than a few people. And Tina didn't want anyone to feel sorry for her. She wasn't angry. She just wanted to skip over her birthday as if it were nothing . . . to sweep it into the past with all the rest of the lame days of her life.

But now she wouldn't have to do that at all.

"Look," Laurie said. "I know this must seem really strange to you, like it's totally coming out of left field or something, but I just want you to know—"

"It doesn't seem strange at all," Tina interrupted shakily. She wiped her face with the palm of her hand. Actually, she thought to herself, it *was* a little strange. In fact, it was a lot strange. A voice inside told her it was too good to be true. But then, Tina was always selling herself short. Why shouldn't she have a big party to celebrate her sixteenth birthday? And why shouldn't Laurie be the one to throw it for her? Tina had shared some amazing times with her, and maybe they'd both grown up enough to appreciate that.

Laurie hesitated. "Are you sure?"

"Yeah, I'm sure," Tina said, laughing through her tears.

"Good," Laurie sounded relieved.

Tina sniffed. "Can I ask you something, though?"

"Of course."

"What does your mom have to say about this?"

Laurie hesitated. "She doesn't know about it. She's going to be out of town."

"Oh." For some reason, the reply hurt a little bit—even though it made perfect sense. Of course Mrs. Penrow didn't know about this. She didn't like Tina, and she never would. Tina couldn't ask for *two* miracles in the same day. It was enough that Laurie was reconciling with her. Besides, Tina didn't need Mrs. Penrow's approval. What did she care what Laurie's mom thought of her?

"So what do you say?" Laurie prodded. "Will you let me do it?"

"Of course," Tina said. "Thanks so much—"

"Oh, this is going to be *great!*" Laurie cried. "I'll plan everything, all right? You won't have to lift a finger. Just give me a list of the people you want to invite, and I'll take it from there."

Tina shook her head. "I don't know what to say," she whispered.

"You've said it all," Laurie answered. Tina could tell by the sound of her voice that she was smiling. "Listen, I better go. But I'll talk to you later, okay?"

"Okay."

"Bye, Tina."

"Bye, Laurie."

There was a click, and the line went dead. Tina clutched the phone tightly. She couldn't move. She simply stared at the plastic in her hand—just to make sure the conversation had been *real*. She went over it again in her mind, replaying it as if it were a cassette. Laurie Penrow was throwing her a party. A Sweet Sixteen. At the grandest, most incredible house in all of North Conroe. With a stable. And a swimming pool. And a hot tub. Tina laughed out loud. She'd not only made a *new* friend this week; she'd won back an old friend. It was like some kind of fairy tale. . . .

Susan. Right. She had to call Susan and give her the news. Immediately. She punched in the number as fast as she could.

Somebody picked up in the middle of the first ring.

"So?" Susan said. "What happened?"

Tina smirked. "How'd you even know it was me?"

"My parents just got caller ID," Susan said impatiently. "So?"

"Got any plans for July twenty-fourth?" Tina asked as offhandedly as possible.

"Uh . . . what's July twenty-fourth?"

Tina grinned. "My birthday, dummy. Thanks for remembering."

"What does that have to do with Laurie Penrow?" Susan asked.

"She's throwing me a party."

"Very funny. Come on, what did she really want?"

Tina started laughing. "I'm serious!" she cried. "Laurie and I are friends again. I don't know why or how . . . or anything, really. I just know that it's true."

"How?" Susan demanded.

Tina's laughter faded. *Whoa.* Susan didn't sound like she was joking around anymore. She sounded very serious all of a sudden. "Uh . . . I just told you," Tina said uncertainly. "She's throwing me a party."

There was silence on the other end.

"What's the matter?" Tina asked.

"This is bad, Tina," Susan said.

Tina laughed again—mostly out of bewilderment. "Why? She said I can invite anyone I want. Don't you get it, Susan? We're gonna have the greatest time ever—"

"Yeah, I get it," Susan interrupted flatly. "*You* don't get it, though."

With that harsh pronouncement every drop of Tina's happiness seemed to flow out of her body—as swiftly as if Susan had pulled a plug in a drain. Why was Susan being such a jerk about this? What was there not to *get?*

"Think about it. Laurie Penrow doesn't talk to you for five years. Then all of a sudden, the day you start tutoring her boyfriend, she's best friends with you again. Doesn't that strike you as a little odd?"

Tina swallowed. Yes, it *was* odd—but the coincidence had been explained. "She and Trent aren't going out anymore," Tina said, almost to herself. "She broke up with him. She said she's been making changes in her life."

Susan laughed coldly. "I'm sure that's what they want you to think," she said.

"They? You're acting like this is a conspiracy. You think Laurie and Trent are both lying to me?" Tina demanded. "It doesn't make any sense. Why would they go through some elaborate scheme just to set me up? Wouldn't they have better things to do with their time?"

"Look, Tina, all I'm saying is that this just doesn't seem right," Susan shot back. "They sat six feet away from us all year and never so much as said hello. Now Trent is reading your haikus and Laurie is throwing you a party? You should be careful before you go jumping into anything that might get you hurt."

Tina shook her head vigorously. "Well, *you* were the one who told me to tutor Trent Rostand in the first place," she protested.

Susan sighed. "I know. . . . Look, I'm not trying to fight with you. But the fact of the matter is that Trent knows you like him. So does Laurie. And Laurie might be mad about it. She might be—"

"But they're *not* going out," Tina argued.

"Or so they told you," Susan said.

"So I *know!*" Tina cried. "I may not spend a lot of time with Laurie Penrow, but I can tell when she's lying, all right? I was pretty much joined at the hip with her for my entire childhood."

"I'm not denying that, Tina. But just step back for a second. I mean, we always talked about Trent Rostand. The thing is, we never thought anything would actually *happen*—"

Tina slammed the phone down on the hook. She was breathing very heavily. She couldn't listen to this. Susan was obviously jealous that Tina was finally enjoying the decent social status they both secretly craved. That was all there was to it. Tina was *not* doing anything wrong. And she certainly wasn't being set up. If Susan wanted to ruin her shot at real happiness, then Susan would just have to stay home the night of July 24.

Laurie

Laurie was just dozing off for a little catnap when Trent showed up.

She couldn't help but be a little irritated. Early afternoon was always *the* most peaceful time of summer. The air was perfectly dry and blazing hot. The back patio was so quiet—nearly silent, in fact, except for the bubbling hot tub or the occasional chirp of a bird. Everything on the Penrow estate shut down for an hour or two. Siesta time: That was how she liked to think of it. The maids and stable hands were on break, so there was no danger of being disturbed by *them*. They ate lunch in the guest kitchen, tucked away on the other side of the house, far from the pool. Yes, lying here in her bikini, she could almost pretend that she was in some far-off, exotic location—like the Italian island of Capri, where she had traveled over spring break. . . .

chapter 12

"We have to talk," Trent said.

Well. So much for fantasy. She sat up straight. Her skin made a sound like Velcro as it peeled off the cushion.

"About what?" she asked dully.

He sat down on the recliner beside her and tossed his book bag onto the ground. "What's wrong?" he asked.

"Nothing," she said. "I was just taking a little nap."

"Sorry."

She shrugged and sighed. Trent would definitely have to start announcing these post-summer-school visits. He should at least call. He was starting to feel just a little too comfortable with showing up here anytime he wanted. But there was no point in starting an argument. "I'm thirsty," she said. "Want some iced tea or something?"

"Sure."

She stretched and stood, then marched past him to the sliding doors that opened onto the game room—a vast, glass-enclosed den equipped with a pool table, pinball machine, and jukebox. The air-conditioning was cranked. The cold air felt very nice against her hot skin. She left the door open for Trent and padded over to a small refrigerator in the corner.

"So?" she asked, grabbing two cans of iced tea.

"So . . . what?"

She frowned and tossed him one of the cans. "So what do you want to talk about? And would you mind closing the door? We have air-conditioning, in case you didn't notice."

"Sorry. Jeez. What's the matter? Are you mad about something?"

"No. It's just . . . this isn't your house."

"I never said it was," he muttered. He slid shut the door and popped open his iced tea. "Sheesh. Anyway, to answer your question, I've been thinking," he said. He took a huge gulp from the can, then set it down on the oak rim of the pool table. "It's about this—"

"Hey!" Laurie protested. Was he *trying* to make her angry? She shook her head and snatched up the can. "That'll leave a circle," she muttered, shoving the drink back into his hand. She studied the wood just to make sure no damage had been done.

He laughed. "What are you gonna do when you actually throw this surprise birthday party? Are you going to, like, hire a personal patrol guy for each guest just to make sure they close doors and use coasters?"

She glared at him. "Well, hopefully nobody will be as rude as you."

He blinked at her. His forehead wrinkled. "All right, *something* is obviously wrong."

"No, it's not," she replied. But something *was* wrong—and until that very moment she hadn't realized what it was. He'd spent every morning this week with *her*. With Tina. And he always looked so chipper and content. Obviously he had to spend time with Tina; otherwise, Laurie's plan wouldn't work. But still . . . did he have to enjoy it so much?

"Well, if it'll make you feel any better, I've come up with a way for you to avoid the stress of dealing with hordes of potentially rude people," he said.

She raised her eyebrows. "Oh yeah? What is it?"

"Call off the party altogether."

"Excuse me?"

"Come on, Laurie, I mean—"

"No, wait a second," she interrupted. Her fingers tightened around her own can. "What are you trying to pull here?"

"I just think you're wrong about Tina," he stated, meeting her gaze. "I'm not trying to hurt you or anything. You *know* that."

"I do? Actually, I'm not so sure." Laurie fought to stay calm. She was not going to let Trent turn her afternoon into a *total* disaster.

He took a deep breath. His face softened a little. "Look, Laurie, I'm not saying that Tina wasn't a jerk to you in the past. But she's *changed*. Really. I mean—"

"I can't *believe* you!" Laurie cried. She turned away from him and began pacing around the room, too frustrated to keep still. "She's got *you* falling for her lame routine, too! After everything I told you . . ."

"What *lame* routine?" he asked.

"She pretends like she's the only person in the world who suffers because she's *sooo* poor and lonely. It's all she ever talks about—" Laurie froze.

Trent was laughing. He was actually *laughing* about this.

"What's so funny?" she barked.

He shook his head and leaned against the glass door. "This is exactly what I mean, Laurie. Maybe she talked about that stuff five years ago, but she doesn't anymore. You know what she talks about now? About how she got into poetry. About how she learned to love Shakespeare—"

Laurie groaned, silencing him. "Not *Shakespeare* again . . ."

"Well, Shakespeare is what *matters,* isn't it? Remember? Summer school? Staying out of the military academy? She's my *tutor,* Laurie!"

"Exactly." She thrust a finger at him. "And for the last time, I'm telling you: The only reason she became your tutor is because she wants to steal you away from me."

He raised his hands, spilling a couple of drops of iced tea on the floor. "Then why hasn't she made a move yet?"

Laurie opened her mouth before she had an answer. "Well . . . I—I don't know," she sputtered. "I'm not a mind reader."

Trent shook his head again and smiled softly. "We don't have to fight about this, Laurie. It's so dumb. You've proved your point. She's not evil. I mean, you gave her the go-ahead to chase after me, and she *still* hasn't done anything. All she did was show me some poem she wrote about me. That's it. If you ask me, I think you guys should be friends."

"Friends?" Laurie cried. "And what poem? Where?"

"I'm telling you, she's a nice girl," he insisted. He turned and opened the door. "Come on. I want to show you something."

Laurie folded her arms across her chest. She refused to budge. She didn't think she could move; she couldn't even pop the top of her drink. She was too frazzled.

"What?" she demanded. Probably some stupid poem by that scheming little brat.

He laughed. "She let me borrow her copy of *The Taming of the Shrew* so Mr. Logan wouldn't think I was a total slacker." He stepped outside and beckoned to

her. "Come on. I promise I'll shut the door behind me."

"You're going to show me a *book?*" Laurie asked.

"Yes!" Trent cried. "Because she filled it with all these notes and underlined all the important passages. She pretty much translated it for me, line by line."

"So what?"

"So that's exactly what you *wanted* her to do." Something in his tone suggested that he was on the verge of adding the word *duh* but thought better of it at the last second. "You wanted her to do my work for me. And she is. She's helping me get a passing grade by—"

"Fine, I'll take a look at the book." She marched out of the house and shut the glass door behind her. Her bare feet slapped loudly on the patio flagstones. All right. She had to get a grip on herself. She was getting worked up for no reason. Obviously Trent needed a little refresher course on what was happening here. Simple. She'd take a look at this book, then talk some sense into him. As calmly as she could, she placed her iced tea down on the side table next to one of the recliners, then sat down and began rummaging through his book bag.

"Uh . . . go ahead and make yourself at home with my stuff," he mumbled sarcastically.

She glanced up at him as he sat back down beside

her. "Likewise. Has it ever occurred to you that you should *ask* before you come over here?"

He didn't say anything.

"I didn't think so." Controlling herself was proving more difficult than expected. Her fingers brushed against a worn paperback. She plucked it from the bag. Sure enough, it was a weather-beaten copy of *The Taming of the Shrew*. Her nose wrinkled. "Eww," she said. It looked like Tina had found it in the garbage. Then again, that wouldn't be a big surprise. Laurie handed it to Trent, clutching it by the spine between her thumb and forefinger as if it were diseased. The pages flapped in the breeze. "Here's your—"

A slip of paper fell out.

"What's this?" Laurie said. She tossed the book on the ground.

Trent frowned. "I have no idea. Tina must have stuck it in there."

"You didn't notice?" she asked suspiciously.

He shrugged. "I hardly had a chance to open the book. Mr. Logan spent the entire period talking about late Renaissance England to give us historical background on it."

Laurie snatched up the paper and began to read aloud: "'Susan Dwyer's four-step program to landing the guy of your dreams. One. Always look him in the eye. If you're feeling brave, bat your lashes. Two. Laugh at his jokes, no matter how awful. . . .'" She giggled once and glanced up at Trent. "What *is* this?"

Trent was smiling, too, but he seemed puzzled. "I have no idea." He reached for it.

"No, no. Hold on." She leaned away from him, clutching the note tightly in both hands. "Are you telling me that you had no idea that this clever little instruction manual was stuck in Tina's book?" She batted her eyelashes, per instruction number one.

He laughed. "Of course not! Do you think Tina would *want* me to find something like that? If she knew . . . well, she'd probably transfer to another school. I'm sure she was passing notes with that friend of hers. . . ."

Without warning, he tried to make a grab for it.

She flinched but managed to dodge his hand and hide the note behind her back. She allowed herself a little grin.

"You were saying?" she asked, raising her eyebrows.

His arm fell limp at his side, but he was still smiling. "Look, I'm sure she left it there by accident, and we have no idea how old it is—could be from last year or something," he said. "I don't—"

"I find that very hard to believe."

"Why?" His smile turned sour. He looked at her as if she were a four-year-old. "*You* found a note that fell out of her book bag. She's obviously absentminded, right?"

Laurie swallowed. She couldn't argue with him on that point, or else she would have to admit that she'd lied to him again. That was the problem with lies: They inevitably came back to haunt you in one way or another.

"Look, just forget this stupid note and everything else for a second," he pleaded. "All I'm asking here is that you *not* throw that birthday party, all right? If you hate her, fine. But it's easier to ignore somebody you hate than to go to all the trouble of humiliating her when . . ." He didn't finish.

"When *what?*"

He threw his hands in the air. "When all she's trying to do is *help* me!"

She smiled. "I can't call off the party, Trent."

"And why not?"

"Because it's too late," she replied evenly. "I already called Tina and told her about it."

"So call her up again. Tell her that you're sorry."

For the first time ever, Trent Rostand didn't look like the most handsome boy on the planet. Hardly. He looked like a fool. He was certainly *acting* like a fool.

"I'm not going to do that," she said.

"Well, then we have a problem," he said.

She nodded. They had a problem, all right. *He* was their problem. So was the fact that he was breaking his word to his own girlfriend. He'd promised he'd help her. Didn't he remember who had kept him in school in the first place? No. Because Tina had brainwashed him.

But Laurie could manage this predicament, too . . . just as she had managed every other one. Oh yes. She would show him who was boss.

"You know, Trent, maybe you shouldn't come to the party," she informed him.

"Fine," he answered.

"Good," she went on in a businesslike manner. "Then we can just break up right now. You can hang out with your little tutor friend, and I can go tell Mrs. Witherspoon that you're cheating by using Tina to get a good grade. And then it's off to military school."

His lips quivered. He stood up. His face was white, etched with disbelief. "Is that what you want?"

She didn't answer. She didn't think she could. Her throat was constricted. What was her problem? Why had she just said that? She didn't want to break up with Trent. She just wanted him to do what he was supposed to. . . .

"Is that what having a boyfriend means to you?" he demanded. "Keeping me in line with threats? Forcing me to do things I don't want to?"

The words ripped into her, but she refused to acknowledge their impact. "You don't understand *anything*, Trent. Having a boyfriend is about making sure he keeps promises he makes. It's about . . ."

She was also going to tell him that having a boyfriend was about making sure he *honors* his girlfriend. But there wasn't much point.

He was already long gone.

Trent

chapter 13

So. Laurie and I sort of patched things up. Actually, what happened was this: I drove around for about three hours straight, totally freaking out at the prospect of losing her forever and of being sent to military school. And then I went back to her house and apologized. I told her that I was sorry for making her so upset. I told her that she has a right to do whatever she wants to do, and if that means throwing a fake party for Tina Vasquez, fine.

In other words, I chickened out.

See, Laurie is really smart. She always wins because she figures out a person's biggest weakness. She knows mine. I scare easily.

And you know what I'm scared of most? Change. People don't like change. They like things the way they are.

I like being at North Conroe High. I like being popular. I like playing JV ball. And I really like having everyone know that the most beautiful girl in school is my girlfriend.

I know Laurie was serious when she said she would get me kicked out of summer school. She's capable of anything. At first, that was one of the reasons I fell in love with her. She lives on her own terms. And she never lets anyone cross her.

But even if I somehow managed to stay at North Conroe and break up with her at the same time, my life would be ruined.

It's so weird: Everybody thinks I have it so great. So they look up to me. I'm one half of North Conroe's "It" couple. And as ridiculous as it sounds, that actually means a lot to me. It means that I'm different from everyone else. If I lost Laurie, I'd lose my mystique. And then people would start wondering if I really *was* different. Even guys like Josh Frederick, good buddies of mine, guys who make fun of me for being Laurie's "slave"— their attitude toward me would change, too. Right now they complain about the fact that I never hang out with them anymore. But if I broke up with Laurie, they wouldn't *want* me to hang out with them. I'd look sort of pathetic, crawling back to my buddies. The dominoes would start tumbling, and pretty soon I'd end up with nothing. I know how North Conroe works.

Okay, there, I said it: Laurie isn't the only person who's scared about what other people think of them. I am, too. But is that really so wrong? Everybody's scared of other people's opinions. In fact, the only person I can think of who *isn't* scared is Tina.

And that's why I hate this whole party thing. I keep hoping that Laurie will prove me wrong, that Tina's evil ways will somehow come to the surface. But the more I hang out with Tina, the more I find I like her. She never tries to act a certain way or put up a front for any reason. She's totally comfortable with who she is. I wish I could say the same for myself. And she doesn't have a crush on me. I know it. So that's one thing I'm sure Laurie is wrong about. And if she's wrong about that, she could be wrong about other stuff.... But I can't let myself think about that.

So, instead of thinking about Laurie, I've been thinking about Tina. A lot. About the way her dark, glossy hair covers her face when she puts her nose in a book (which is almost all the time). About the way her laugh can fill an empty classroom. I've even thought about those little sparkly barrettes she wears sometimes. But don't get me wrong—I think about the important stuff, too, like how she helps me with my work. She's probably the smartest person I've ever met. And the most creative. She even got *me* to write a haiku:

> Hitting the last shot
> at the buzzer—swish! is like
> a glimpse of heaven.

I know it's weak. But that's not the point. The point is that Tina is getting me to try all sorts of different things, to use my brain in ways I never have before. What happened to me this past year—when did I stop caring about school, about thinking for myself? It seems like it happened right around the time I met Laurie—but is that just a coincidence? And why is it that Tina can make me feel so alive, like I'm really thinking, moving on with my life, going somewhere . . . ?

On the other hand, I've only known Tina a couple of weeks. The fact of the matter is that I still know Laurie a lot better.

Which brings me back to the same issue all over again: Knowing Laurie, do I really want to go out with her?

Yes, I do. And no, I don't. Since I can't make up my mind, I take the easy way out—by doing nothing at all. I go to summer school. I have a blast with Tina. And then I go hang out with Laurie as she plans Tina's doom. At least I manage to stay out of the actual planning process. Whoopee. I'm a real saint, aren't I?

Tina

I keep expecting to wake up. I keep thinking that this entire month has been some kind of incredible, never-ending dream . . . a dream Shakespeare might have written about. Seriously. How can circumstances change so fast? How could the most potentially depressing birthday of my life turn out to be the greatest day ever?

All right . . . I'm getting ahead of myself. The party hasn't even happened yet. But judging from the way things are going with Laurie and the way things are going with Trent, I must say, I'm pretty confident that the entire affair will rule. I mean, come on: swimming, horseback riding, dancing—what more could a girl ask for?

Every single time I talk to Laurie on the phone, I hang up in shock. We laugh. We tell each other jokes. She asks about my friends. She asks my opinion about all kinds of things, especially about movies. She says she trusts my judgment because I'm a film buff. I mean, she even asks me about my poetry. My poetry! It's like she's really making the effort to get to know me because she never gave herself the chance before. I can't believe how wrong I was about her. I'm just upset that five whole years went down the drain. But we have the rest of our lives to make up for it. I'm not going to blow our friendship this time.

And the most incredible part of all?

Trent Rostand's personality is actually *more* amazing than I imagined.

When you build somebody up in your mind for an entire year, you kind of expect to be disappointed. I have to be honest . . . I'm not one hundred percent over my crush. But the funny thing is, I've completely resigned myself to the fact that we'll never go out. And I'm totally cool with it. (Well, maybe that's a slight exaggeration.) But I know that he would never think of me that way. Anyway, I can't bring myself to do something that might hurt Laurie—not after all she's done. Susan was right: Dreaming about somebody's boyfriend is one thing, but actually going after him is another. It's not right.

Laurie claims she's over him, of course. But she's just saying that. Feelings still linger. Especially powerful ones. It's obvious *he* still has feelings for her. And I know from my own experience that the pain of a breakup can take a long time to heal, even if it's just a breakup between friends. I mean, I'm still not *completely* comfortable with Laurie. Not like the way we were when we were eleven. There's still a little awkwardness. But we're getting there.

So all in all, summer has been very sweet indeed.

There's only one little element of sourness. Actually, it's a fairly big element, but I try not to think about it too hard. I still haven't made up with Susan. It's so stupid. I mean, I can barely remember why we fought. But since I'm such a stubborn jerk, I keep waiting for *her* to call. I'm sure she's doing the exact same thing.

Oh, well. At least I know she's going to be at the party. Laurie told me that every single person on my list RSVP'd yes.

I'll make up with her then. I swear.

Hooray! Here's to turning sixteen! And to the most amazing night of my life.

Laurie

Have you ever had one of those really annoying pimples that just won't go away? You know, some big, huge, red monster zit—right smack on your chin or on the tip of your nose? So that everyone can see it? And whisper about it when you're not around? "Oh my God, that girl has *got* to get some Oxy 10 in a major way."

Well, that's exactly what Tina Vasquez is to me. Exactly. It's the perfect . . . what's the word? Metaphor? Analogy? Something like that. The point is, she's been a blemish on my existence for five whole years now, nearly a third of my life. No matter how much zit medicine or cover-up I put on, she still manages to stick around.

So I'm just going to have to pop her.

On a completely unrelated topic, I think I'm getting an ulcer. I'm not joking. I feel sick to my stomach all the time. It's Trent's fault. Spending time with him is like hanging out with a corpse. He's so cold. He doesn't do anything. He doesn't say anything. We barely talk. He hasn't even kissed me in a month.

But we're still together, and that's what counts. Our relationship will get back to where it was before. I know it will. He's smart. He knows that we need each other. Breaking up is an empty threat: He would never do it. We're the king and queen of North Conroe. Royalty doesn't split. I mean, look what happened to Princess Di and Prince Charles when *they* broke up. Disaster. Scandal. Tragedy. When they split apart, they lost everything.

And that's what would happen to us. The very fact that we're going out is what makes us royalty.

I don't want to take any chances, though. I've learned my lesson about lying. It never works. It's best just to keep the truth hidden and not say anything at all. So I haven't told Trent about my *real* plan for the night of the twenty-fourth. As much as it sickens me, I have to acknowledge that there's a chance he would tell Tina.

I still have a hard time figuring out how I even *got* to this place—this ridiculous point in my life where I have to teach my own boyfriend the truth about Tina Vasquez. I mean, the entire mess started with my trying to *help* Trent.

All I ever wanted to do was help.

But people have never understood that about me. I'm probably the most misunderstood person I know. It's true. Nobody ever understood what Tina put me through, either. Nobody knows that I really did like her when we were kids. Really. I just knew that we could never be truly close, the way she wanted. If she had just been cool about it and accepted the fact that we could say hi to each other in the halls but that we couldn't hang out in certain situations, we could have avoided all this. But no. She had to make me feel guilty and embarrass me, only because I've wanted what's *natural*.

Everyone wants to be on the winning team. And once Trent realizes that Tina will never make the cut, we'll be back to normal.

Trent

chapter 14

The moment Trent stepped inside Laurie's open front door, he felt like turning around and bolting. An enormous banner was stretched across the entire length of the Penrows' front hall, perched over the sweeping marble spiral staircase that led to the second floor.

Happy Sweet 16, Tina!

He had to hand it to his girlfriend: She'd spared no expense. The letters were at least three feet high. She was the consummate hostess. His head drooped. A miracle could always intervene on Tina's behalf, right? Maybe nobody would show. Maybe there'd be some kind of freak tropical storm, or an earthquake, or a tornado. Or maybe Laurie's parents would have to cut their trip short . . .

Laurie stepped through the doorway.

He held his breath. Maybe he should just tell her that he wouldn't go through with it. Maybe he should finally have the courage to *act* on his feeling for once—

"Is *that* what you're wearing?" she asked.

Trent blinked. The question took him by surprise. What was this, a formal occasion? He'd thought it was going to be a swimming-and-riding party. A hang-around-outside-and-get-dirty party. That was why he'd deliberately dressed down—digging up an old pair of paint-stained jeans and a ripped black T-shirt that was several sizes too big.

But then, he should have remembered: Laurie hated that kind of grungy attire. All the Penrows did. No matter *what* the circumstances.

"What's the matter?" he asked.

Laurie grimaced. She, of course, was fully decked out in makeup and a designer black dress that probably cost half as much as her car. In fact, she looked more beautiful than ever, which for some reason only made him very depressed.

"Just get back into your car and go home, all right?" she grumbled. She glanced at her watch. "It's not even eight. People won't start getting here for at least another half hour. You can change and be back here by nine. Fashionably late. With the emphasis on *fashionably.*"

"But I thought . . ." He didn't even know what he wanted to say. There was no *way* he would go home just to change.

Her lips pressed into a tight line. "I thought we agreed not to fight," she said.

"I'm not fighting!" he hollered over the music.

She shook her head and laughed. "Whatever. I've got things to do." She disappeared back outside.

"I . . . ," he began to protest, but stopped. Great. But in a way, he was glad he had dressed like a bum. It would be the lone victory he would have over her tonight, so he knew he had better savor it. Talk about depressing. It was *pitiful*. Getting on her nerves was the closest he could come to taking a stand against her. He slumped down at the foot of the marble staircase. *Man.* He was worse than a marionette. He was a coward—a spineless, sniveling coward.

Laurie suddenly reappeared. "Can you give me a hand and help set up?"

He stared at her as she hurried down a corridor toward the kitchen. He'd helped her "set up" plenty already. He'd set up Tina, hadn't he? By keeping his mouth shut, he'd collaborated with Laurie. "Hey, Laurie, can I ask you something?" he called.

"I don't see why not," she called back. Cabinet doors slammed. "Do you think you can talk and move at the same time, though?"

His eyes smoldered. He pushed himself to his feet

but remained by the stairwell. "What are you planning on doing to Tina tonight? I mean, *exactly?*"

Laurie briskly marched back through the front hall, carrying a huge plastic bowl and an unopened bag of potato chips. "You'll see," she replied, without even pausing to glance at him. She vanished out the door again.

"Why don't you just tell me?" he demanded.

She didn't answer.

That's it. Enough. He stormed after her, running down the front walk. He managed to catch up to her on the driveway—and he grabbed her arm. She shook free.

"Do you *mind?*" she growled.

"I just want to—"

"I'm not telling you, Trent," she interrupted, whirling to face him. "For all you know, I might not do anything at all. Maybe I decided to be nice to Tina. Or maybe I didn't. Either way, you won't know until it's too late."

Trent shook his head. His mind raced, searching for the right response—anything to upset her, to get her to reveal the truth. But she was already walking calmly around the garage to the back patio. Maybe he could just wait by the front door for Tina and warn her when she arrived. But no . . . Laurie would just deny everything, and with no evidence to disprove her, *he'd* end up looking like a liar. Worse. A lunatic. If he wanted things

to stay the same, if he wanted to keep his status at North Conroe—or even *be* at North Conroe—he had to go along with Laurie's plan. Either way, Laurie won. She'd beaten him. His shoulders slumped. Very slowly, he walked back toward the house.

By nine o'clock the party was officially on its way out of control.

It was going to be one of those ragers that people would talk about for years: a house-trashing, heat-of-the-summer, blowout bash. The entire teenage population of North Conroe was either here or on its way. A hundred kids must have been packed into the first floor of Laurie's house. Dozens more were spilling out by the pool. A few of the very rambunctious ones had already jumped in the water. The stereo was cranked on full volume, and the walls were shaking with some rap song: *Boom . . . ba-boom . . . boom . . . ba-boom. . . .* Trent could feel the beat in his teeth. People were dancing. People were shouting. He was also happy to note that people were leaving doors open and putting their drinks on top of any surface they could find—varnished wood, TV sets, even the computer.

Well, at the very least, Laurie would have a miserable time cleaning up tomorrow.

So where was the guest of honor?

A faint spark of hope began to flicker inside him. Maybe Tina wouldn't come. He searched room after room, snaking his way through the crowd, craning his neck. And even though he saw lots of Tina's friends (at least, he *assumed* they were her friends because he didn't know them—and they looked very uncomfortable), she was nowhere to be found. By the time he'd gone through the entire house twice and wound up back in the front hall, he was sure Tina was missing. Strange: It had never occurred to him that she would blow off her own birthday party. But maybe she had gotten wise to Laurie's real intentions. Maybe she was even smarter than he'd given her credit for—

"Trent Rostand! Dude, are you avoiding me?"

Oh, brother. Not now. He knew the scratchy sound of Josh Frederick's voice even before he saw that signature red baseball cap bobbing down the spiral staircase. He had to smile, though. It figured Josh would go upstairs. There was a sign taped to the banister: Nobody Allowed on the Second Floor! Some people were put on this earth for the sole purpose of breaking rules. *Any* rules.

"What's up, man?" Josh asked. There was a mischievous glint in his green eyes. He gave Trent a quick, puzzled once-over. "You really dress to impress, huh?"

He rolled his eyes. Josh would be a good match for Laurie. They both put *way* too much emphasis on appearances. "What were you doing upstairs?" he asked.

"Just taking a little tour. I almost got lost. This house is *insane*."

"Yeah," Trent mumbled. "So are the people who live in it."

The words floated right past Josh. "So who's this Tina chick, anyway?" he asked, glancing up at the banner. "Is she, like, a friend of Laurie's from out of town or something?"

"She's in our grade, Josh. She goes to our school."

Josh frowned at him. "Then how come I've never heard of her?"

Because you're just like me, Trent wanted to answer. *Because you don't notice anyone outside your own clique.* But instead he just shrugged and said, "She's kind of quiet."

"Hmmm." Josh stroked his chin, grinning. "Why do I get the feeling that there's something you're not telling me? Why did Laurie become friends with her all of a sudden?"

There were a hundred possible answers Trent could give to that question: Laurie's revenge, her pride . . . but none were ones he particularly felt like sharing, and all of them made him feel ill. So he shrugged again.

"She's my tutor," he said.

Josh raised his eyebrows. "Your tutor?"

As if on cue, Tina stepped through the front door.

Oh my God...

Trent's eyes widened.

She looked *incredible*.

What was going on here? She was wearing a black spaghetti-strap dress that clung to her hips and hung just past her knees. She never wore dresses. And he'd never noticed how slim and delicate she was; in class, she always wore baggy T-shirts and jeans or those big overalls. Her hair was down, too: parted in the middle, framing her dark features—she tilted up her head as she laid eyes on the banner.

"Is that *her?*" Josh whispered.

Trent nodded, stupefied.

Josh leaned close to him. "Now I understand."

"Understand what?"

"Why Laurie became friends with her. Ever notice how gorgeous chicks always hang out together? It's like they want to keep an eye on the competition."

Trent scowled at him. That was the most ridiculous thing he'd ever heard—especially given the real circumstances. But Josh didn't notice. He was too busy staring at Tina.

"Nice. Very nice," Josh murmured, looking Tina up and down like a wolf. "Is she seeing anybody?" he asked.

Suddenly his friend was making him very sick. Now would probably be a good time to end this conversation. Trent turned away and marched right over to Tina.

"Hey, there," he said.

She smiled and seemed unable to tear her gaze from the banner. She blinked a few times and swallowed. Her eyes moistened. "Hi, Trent. I'm so glad you're here."

"Where else would I be?" Trent asked, trying to meet her eyes. But she wouldn't look at him. She must be really nervous.

"You know, Trent, I was thinking about something. Do you know that if it weren't for you, I wouldn't be here right now? I mean, none of this would be happening. You brought Laurie back into my life." She stopped and looked at him.

Trent's face fell. What was she saying?

"I mean, look at this party." Tina motioned with her hand at the huge living room, now filling with dancing kids. "This is all your doing. If it hadn't been for that day at LotsaFunland—"

"Tina . . ." He had to stop her. She was being so sincere, and he didn't know what to say in return. In that

instant he felt like he was drowning, struggling to reach the surface, being tossed around by forces beyond his control. And the strangest part of all was that he was *angry*. At himself, for being such a wimp. And at her. At Tina, the victim—for showing up, for making him feel like such a jerk, for suddenly deciding to be so beautiful when she'd spent years hiding behind that plain facade—

"What's the matter?" she said softly.

"Why did you get so dressed up?" he found himself demanding. The inexplicable anger swallowed everything else inside him: the guilt, the shame, but most of all, any ability to think rationally.

She laughed, but it wasn't her usual warm, sunny laugh. She sounded cool, like a tinkle of ice. "It's my party, isn't it, Trent? Wasn't I supposed to dress up? Or wasn't that part of the *plan?*"

Trent bit his lip. What did she mean by "plan"—and why was she acting so strange? She kept using his name, saying it in a harsh way. She was acting like someone else. . . . She was acting like Laurie. How could he let this happen? Of course. Now that Tina was hanging out with Laurie so much, she wanted to become just like her. And she was doing a pretty good job. But Trent didn't like it. *Because,* he realized, *I don't like Laurie very much anymore.*

His eyes darted around the room. By now everyone was stealing glances at Tina, whispering. Most of them were probably asking themselves the same question Josh had: *Who is this gorgeous girl, and how come I've never heard of her?*

"What's the matter, Trent?" Tina said.

Tell her, you wimp! a voice screamed inside him. *Tell her that this whole thing is a sham! Tell her to turn around and run home as fast as she can to just be herself again. She doesn't need these people. Tell her she's beautiful and that you're falling in love with her. . . .*

"I'm fine," he heard himself answer. "Why?"

"Well, you haven't even wished me happy birthday yet," she teased.

He swallowed. He couldn't even manage *that*. Why couldn't he save her from this terrible night? Why couldn't he—

"Well, I'm going to go find Laurie, okay?" she said, patting his shoulder. "Maybe she'll like my new dress better than you." She started to walk away, only to stop a second later. She looked back over her shoulder and added, "Oh, and Trent? Thanks again for making this happen. I'm sure this will be a night I won't ever forget."

And then she was gone, swallowed up by the crowd—off to find the girl who was about to ruin her life.

"Hey, dude?" Josh called to him. "If she's not seeing anybody, put in a good word for you-know-who, all right?"

Trent nodded. But the gesture wasn't in response to Josh's asinine request. No, he was nodding because he suddenly realized another reason he'd been angry with Tina. Until now she had been his little secret, almost like a genie in a bottle. Not anymore, though. By dressing up, by allowing her inner beauty to reach the surface, she'd let out the secret. All of a sudden everyone was noticing the incredible girl who had always been there, unseen, right in their midst.

Right at the very moment Trent was going to lose her forever.

Tina

chapter 15

"Go, go, go, go . . ."

Tina had to hold back not to press her hands against her ears. The music was so loud. And everything was happening so fast. Yet she couldn't move. She couldn't *think*. How could anyone stand the stereo speakers so *loud?* She glanced around the darkened living room, squinting at the mob of gyrating strangers. Funny: Right now she felt less like a sixteen-year-old and more like her own grandmother. *"I just don't understand how you young kids can listen to that music. I don't understand how one word repeated a million times over the same deafening drumbeat can send you into a frenzy."*

Maybe the problem was that she'd never heard this song before. She could pretty much guess its name, though. Yes. Judging from the fascinating lyrical content, it must be called "Go."

"Go, go, go, go . . ."

All her life, it seemed, Tina had been waiting to be invited to a party like this one—one of those legendary "ragers" thrown by North Conroe's social elite. But she was beginning to see that she hadn't missed much . . . not unless going deaf and being jostled and feeling utterly lost counted as having a great time. Was this typical? It was definitely *not* the scene she'd envisioned while fretting over her hair and makeup earlier in the evening. Naively enough, she had imagined strolling triumphantly back into the Penrows' fabulous home after her five-year exile—at which point Laurie and Trent and various other beautiful people would swarm around her and break into a rousing rendition of "Happy Birthday."

"Go, go, go, go . . ."

That's just want she wanted to do. Go. Go home and hide under the covers. Go away from this whole scene, from this whole night. But she couldn't. She was going to stay right here and see it out. Show them all that she was just as good as the rest of them. No . . . better.

The night had started just as she had planned. She'd spent hours getting ready—her makeup and hair had to be just right. She and her mother had started at 6 P.M. with the preparations: first a long, relaxing bath, then her nails would need to be done while her mother set her hair. Tina had never had the chance to play Cinderella before, and it was fun. And although she loved having her mother's help, she couldn't help but miss her best friend, Susan. It would have been perfect if Sue had been there, critiquing every step of the way, being her usual sarcastic self.

But Tina couldn't let that little snag ruin the night. Everything was going to be perfect. Besides, Susan must be here somewhere, and Tina was sure they could put their little fight behind them. Once Susan saw that her fears about Laurie were wrong, maybe all three of them could be friends.

This was her night to shine, her coming-out party, her Sweet Sixteen. And maybe this would be the night something would happen with Trent, even just a little something. Or was that too much to hope for? Had she been wrong about her feelings for him, or was he feeling it, too—the attraction she felt as she sat next to him every morning, talking about books, about movies, about . . . everything.

Yes, tonight was the night that would make it all perfect. When she and her mother had finished with the hair, the makeup, and the nails, Tina slipped into the new black dress her mother had bought for just this occasion. It was expensive, more than they could afford.

"Honey, it's your birthday. You deserve to feel special," her mother had said. And she did. She felt special; she looked special. She almost didn't know her own reflection when she looked in the mirror. Could it be true, what Susan was always telling her? That she was more beautiful than Laurie would ever be? She didn't want to compete with Laurie—they were friends now, and Tina wanted to keep it that way. But when she looked in the mirror tonight, she couldn't help thinking that maybe there was some truth to it; maybe she really wasn't the ugly duckling she thought she was. Maybe she was finally a swan.

When she left the house, she was walking on air. She had just gotten her driver's license, and already her mother was letting her use the car. She slid into the driver's seat—it didn't matter that the car was ten years old and a bit on the rusty side. She still felt like a princess. She threw her bag in the passenger seat—she'd brought along some jeans and a pair of boots for later. Laurie had promised them all a midnight ride on the family's beautiful horses, and Tina wanted to join in. But she couldn't ride a horse in this dress. Or maybe she could! It was up to her—the night was hers, and she was free to do whatever she wanted.

On the drive to Laurie's, all she could think about was Trent. It was wrong to feel this way about her friend's ex, and she knew it. But maybe after he and Laurie had been broken up for a while—who knew what might happen? A girl could dream, couldn't she? Especially on her sixteenth birthday.

She arrived at Laurie's at eight on the dot. There were only a few cars in the long driveway. Was she too early? What if nobody showed up? Suddenly anxiety replaced her giddiness. Maybe she should just drop her stuff in the barn first, stretch her legs, calm down a little. She grabbed her bag and headed across the lawn to the barn.

Tina shuddered to think of it now. A shiver ran up her spine, even though she stood in a room packed with hot, dancing bodies. What if she hadn't gone out to the barn and found what she had found? What if she . . .

"*There* you are!" Susan cried over the music, yanking her from her thoughts.

Before Tina had a chance to react, Susan grabbed her by the arm and whisked her around the corner to a small, empty foyer.

"Where have you been?" Susan hissed, glancing furtively in each direction. "I've been looking all over for you. You were supposed to be here at eight, weren't you?"

Tina blinked a few times. *Wow.* Susan really must have missed her during this past month. "I . . . uh, there was something I had to take care of . . . ," Tina started.

"Listen, Tina, something's wrong." Susan seized her by the shoulders. "Trent and Laurie are still going out."

"Oh, really?" Tina said sarcastically. But Susan didn't notice her tone—she just kept right on talking.

"It's true. I heard Laurie talking to somebody in the kitchen. She was saying how she was planning on surprising Trent with a road trip to Mexico at the end of the summer—"

"Whoa, whoa, slow down, Susan," Tina interrupted, laughing. She had missed her best friend, and right now she was the only person Tina wanted to talk to.

"Just listen to me!" Susan whispered. "She wasn't talking about Trent in the past tense. She was talking about the *future*."

Tina sighed. "Look, you don't have anything to worry about. I have it all under control."

But Susan started shaking her head before Tina had even finished. "No, you aren't listening to me. I know we fought, and I know you think I'm jealous or I'm out to ruin your good time, but that's not it. Look, I can't put my finger on it exactly, but there's something weird going on here." Susan stopped to take a breath for a second.

"Are you done? Because I have something to tell you," Tina whispered, pulling Susan in closer.

"Bu-But . . . this . . . ," Susan sputtered—then gasped as Tina abruptly backed away from her.

Laurie was rounding the corner.

Here we go, Tina thought, bracing herself. Now they could put an end to this nonsense once and for all.

"Hey!" Laurie cried. "So *this* is where you've been hiding. Happy birthday!"

Susan cocked her eyebrow at Tina, her way of asking, *What is going on here?*

"Thanks, Laurie," Tina said as calmly as she could. "This party is so incredible. You really . . ." She paused.

Laurie was frowning, looking Tina up and down and shaking her head.

"Is something the matter?" Tina asked.

"No, not at all," Laurie said. "It's just . . . that's a great dress. Where did you get it?"

"My mom gave it to me for tonight," Tina answered, doing a jokey little pirouette. "She wanted me to have something special for such a special occasion. Do you really like it?"

Laurie smiled. "Absolutely."

"Do you know my friend Susan?" Tina asked. "She's—"

"Mm-hmm," Laurie said, without so much as a

glance in Susan's direction. She slipped her hand under Tina's arm and began dragging her down the hall.

Uh-oh. Tina shot a quick, apologetic grin over her shoulder—but Susan clearly wasn't happy. In fact, she almost looked pale. Tina wished she had had the time to explain. But in a few minutes Susan would know what was going on. Everyone would know.

"Where are you taking me?" Tina asked, although she was sure she already knew the answer.

"You'll see," Laurie answered with a wink, leading Tina through the game room and out onto the pool patio. "Come on, people!" she suddenly called. "We're meeting at the stables!"

Tina stumbled after Laurie into the darkness of the backyard. The invitations mentioned a midnight ride, but it wasn't even nine-thirty. Tina had thought she would have more time . . . but it seemed that Laurie was anxious to get the party under way. And who was Tina to stop her?

"Are we going to ride right now?" she asked tentatively.

"You'll see," Laurie answered again.

Tina tried to slow down, but Laurie kept yanking her along across the grass. She laughed, mostly because she was overwhelmed and scared. Scared of what was waiting in the stables. She shivered again. A soft breeze was

blowing. It *was* perfect riding weather. So sad to think they wouldn't be going anywhere. Tina was suddenly gripped with fear. She'd thought she could do this, but maybe she couldn't. She needed to catch her breath, to think.

"Maybe I should change or something," she said, hoping to stall Laurie for a few more minutes. They were far enough from the house now so that she could hear the crickets over the thumping music.

"Into what?" Laurie asked. "You don't have any riding clothes, right?"

No, I don't, Tina thought. *I don't because I threw them in the back of the car on my way home about an hour ago. After I saw what you have set up in the stables for me. But I came back. And I'm ready to face this,* she told herself. *I'm ready to face this.*

"After this, I bet you won't even *think* about horses," Laurie soothed. "It's that good."

Tina shrugged as calmly as she could, but her heart was pounding. She glanced back at the house. Lots of shadowy figures were beginning to make their way across the lawn. This *was* going to be big. Maybe too big. Did she really know what she was doing?

Laurie finally let go of her arm when they reached the stables: a cute little barnlike structure built of worn

red wood that was about the size of Tina's entire house. When Tina was eleven, the Penrows owned five horses. Now that number had doubled.

Laurie pushed open the door with a whiny creak. The pungent odor of hay and manure wafted out at them as she flipped on the light. Tina followed her across the straw-covered floor to the first stall. Everything was happening in slow motion. She could barely stand up straight, her legs were shaking so badly. Her eyes narrowed. It was just as she had found it earlier tonight. The little open room was empty except for a couple of bales of hay and—of all things—a TV and VCR, sitting on top of a little folding card table.

Tina was ready. "Movies?" she said, trying to keep her voice light.

"Well, I know you're such a film buff," Laurie answered in that same cheerful tone. "So I decided to make a little movie in honor of your birthday."

"Really? Wow, I can't wait." Tina felt almost hysterical. She heard her voice catch and almost started to cry. *Keep it together, keep it tougher,* she told herself. Laurie had gone to so much trouble to do this—it made Tina sick to think of all the planning that had gone into this night. And for what? Why?

Tina mustered her strength to ask one question she

was actually curious about. "Um, why are you showing it to me out here?"

Laurie leaned close to her. "I had to hide the setup from certain people," she whispered.

Tina kept right on smiling—but in the back of her head a crazy thought was starting. Maybe Trent wasn't in on it. Trent didn't know. Laurie set this up out here to keep it from him. But Trent still had to know some of what was going on—he *had* to. Tina didn't have time to think it all through right now. The stable began to fill with kids.

Once again Tina's heart started to pound. She didn't know how much more suspense she could handle. People closed in on her, forcing her and Laurie to edge closer and closer to the television. Some faces she recognized; some she didn't. It was a good thing she didn't suffer from claustrophobia.

The volume inside the building rose. It was clear that the guests were baffled. Tina stood on her tiptoes, straining to see Trent, but he was nowhere in sight. Could it be that he had no idea what Laurie had planned? She had to know how much he had been involved.

"Can I have your attention, please!" Laurie called.

A hush fell over the crowd.

"I want to thank you all for coming out here," Laurie announced. "Many of you probably don't know the birthday girl, Tina Vasquez. So to get you all better acquainted with her, I decided to make a short movie. A sort of documentary biography, like those shows they have on A & E. Enjoy." She leaned over and flicked on the TV, then pressed play.

Tina held her breath. The stable was silent. A documentary? How could she say that? Tina forced a smile. She couldn't imagine why or how Laurie could have become so heartless, so cruel. Her heart was beating so fast that she was worried she might keel over. She shot a quick glance at Laurie, but Laurie was staring intently at the screen.

There was a brief burst of static, then the tape started. It showed two young girls, maybe around eight or nine years old. The video wasn't very high quality, but you could still tell the girls were at an amusement park—it was LotsaFunland, virtually unchanged from seven years ago.

"Hello, there!" the blond girl said into the camera. She was skinny and small, with big silver braces and frizzy, shoulder-length hair. "I'm Laurie, and this is my bestest best friend, Tina-Tina Bo Beana!"

The familiar old nickname sent a piercing blade

through Tina's heart. She hadn't heard that in years. She looked over at Laurie and saw that her eyes were glued to the screen. Her mouth was open as if she was in shock, gulping for air.

The camera cut over to the other little girl, nine-year-old Tina. Same haircut, same big smile, just a little smaller than she was now. And just as shy. "Hi," she said quietly, waving at the camera and out to the room of people watching the video.

The camera cut back to Laurie, still talking, babbling, really. She was showing off her ballet moves for the camera and saying: "When I grow up, I'm going to be a prima ballerina!" Then she stood with her hands on her hips in front of the camera, her neon T-shirt, with the huge name of a long forgotten rap star emblazoned across it, almost filling the screen.

A few giggles went up from behind Tina. The kids from the party didn't know what to make of this old home video. It certainly wasn't very flattering to the hostess. As a matter of fact, it was downright hilariously embarrassing.

Suddenly one guy called out, "Hey, Laurie, didn't know you were such a big Vanilla Ice fan!"

"Yeah, 'Ice, Ice, baby,'" another girl sang out, followed by a huge wave of laughter.

Tina looked over at Laurie, but she was just standing stock-still, staring at the screen. "What . . . how . . . this isn't the tape . . . ," Laurie hissed.

The image on the screen changed. It was the two little girls again, this time outside at the Penrows' pool. Tina was wearing her old red tank swimsuit—just seeing it again brought a smile to her face; she had loved that suit. Then the camera panned over to Laurie on the diving board, screeching, "Watch me, Mommy, watch me, watch me dive, Mommy, watch me. . . ." Laurie was skinny, flat chested, and decked out in a tacky neon bikini. She grinned widely at the camera, showing off her huge braces and fluffing up her frizzy blond hair.

"Hey, Laurie, is that your ugly twin, or is that really you?" someone called out. Again the barn erupted in laughter.

With this round of laughs the spell seemed to be broken. Laurie snapped and lunged for the VCR. "That's not the right tape! That's not what you were supposed to see. . . ." She was furiously pressing buttons, trying to stop the tape. She hit the rewind key, and everyone watched the tape again as it wheeled backward. On the screen Laurie's skinny little body appeared to dive backward out of the pool.

"Watch me dive, Mommy," someone mimicked in a

falsetto from the room, and the giggles went up again.

"Hey, I was watching that! Put it back on!" Tina recognized the voice as Susan's, and for the first time all night a genuine smile crossed her face.

Tina took a deep breath and leaned over to Laurie as she crouched in front of the VCR. "I was actually on time for the party. But I came in here first to drop off my riding clothes. I found your little video 'documentary,' Laurie. And I watched it. But I didn't think it covered the whole story, so I thought your friends might like to see this video instead. I didn't think you'd mind. After all, it is my *birthday*."

"You are going to be so sorry—," Laurie screeched, and lunged at her. Suddenly Trent was between them, holding Laurie back.

"Whoa, what's going on here?" he said.

"I think I can explain," Tina said.

"Then why don't you, you little two-faced sneak?" Laurie spat out.

Everyone in the stable was frozen. They looked like a bunch of clothing store mannequins. A path was still cleared from the stall to the door, where Trent had cut through the crowd, as if invisible barriers had been erected, dividing the crowd in half. A few kids were still laughing . . . but others were definitely unsure of how to react. Some were staring at their feet. Others were actually upset. It was pretty clear that Laurie would never have let any of them see that unflattering video if it had been up to her. Who was running this party?

"I don't think I have anything to say to you," Tina said to Laurie. "Or to you, for that matter," she added, looking right at Trent. "And to the rest of you, thanks for coming to my birthday party." Tina's voice was shaking, but she didn't cry. "It's been a blast."

Tina held her head high as she cut through the crowd, knowing that everyone was watching her leave. In her head the song from earlier in the night was still playing . . . *go, go, go*. And once she got outside the barn door, that's just what she did—breaking into a run, she sprinted for her car just as the tears started to run down her face.

Laurie

Laurie just stood there in shock, watching Tina walk out of the barn. If Trent hadn't been holding her arms, she surely would have run after her—screaming, tearing, punching. She couldn't believe the anger that was inside her right now.

When the door closed behind Tina, any last traces of laughter in the room died. Laurie closed her eyes and wished hard that she were somewhere else. When she opened her eyes, though, she was still there, with a roomful of people staring at her. And her guests looked like they wished they were somewhere else, too.

This was just great. Tina and Trent had managed to ruin her party. But maybe it could be fixed. Maybe she could find the right tape, the one she had made, not Tina's trick tape. If she could show that to everyone, they would know what a dork Tina was. And when it was all over, five minutes from now, Trent would look

chapter 16

back on his misguided feelings for Tina and wince. . . .

"What is going on?" Trent asked her now, shaking her by the shoulders. "What was the deal with that old home video? Was that your idea?" His eyes darted around the stable. They came to rest on Laurie. "Why did you do that? You know you only embarrassed yourself."

"I didn't do it, stupid," Laurie hissed at him. "Yes, I made a video for tonight, but it wasn't that one. Mine was just a little joke; a parody about Tina's stupid life. . . ." She had to smile a little, thinking of it. It had been so perfect. Only a few minutes long but damaging enough to ruin that little brat forever.

The video she had made was very different from the one her guests saw. It started with a great title:

Tina Vasquez: Portrait of a Loser

The image cut to another handwritten placard:

Introductory Haiku

Hi. I'm a loser.

My name is Tina Vasquez.

See how lame I am.

Then a photograph suddenly appeared: an awful, hideous picture of Tina from the sixth-grade yearbook, the one that had been taken only days after she'd recovered from a bout of chicken pox. Her face was dotted with bright red scabs.

And there was more: handheld shots of the crumpled note Susan had written Tina: "Susan Dwyer's Four-Step Program to Landing the Guy of Your Dreams," along with a few other unflattering photos and the other note Laurie had found in the trash.

Laurie had been so proud of herself; for a video novice, she had to say her little movie had turned out pretty well. But now no one would see it, and instead they had all seen the video that Tina had put in its place—the video of her humiliating "awkward" stage, as her mother liked to call it.

"Wait, are you telling me that Tina found out what you were up to and switched the tapes?" Trent asked. "How . . . ?"

"Why don't you tell me, Trent." Laurie glared at him. "There's only one way she could have known. There was only one other person in on this. *You*."

"But I didn't even know what you were planning to do—you wouldn't tell me, remember? No, I didn't tell Tina. But I wish I had." Trent shook his head and smiled a little. "It doesn't matter now. That video . . . Tina's video of the two of you; it was classic." He started to laugh. "And just what you deserve." He let go of Laurie's arms and turned to walk out.

"Where do you think you're going?" Laurie asked.

Trent stood in the doorway, half turned toward Laurie, half turned outside.

"Don't tell me you're going after her." Laurie groaned.

Everybody was glancing between the two of them now. Laurie held her breath. If Trent *did* leave, then Laurie would have a lot of explaining to do on his behalf. People would start to wonder why he cared so much about a girl they had never even heard of until tonight. Rumors would fly.

But if he just took a moment to reflect, to really *think* about what it would mean to abandon Laurie Penrow . . . then everything would work out just fine.

"Remember, I'm the one you should be worried about. She humiliated me in front of everyone. I mean, it's not like she would have been invited to any more parties after this one. She's used to this kind of—"

"What did Tina do to you, anyway?" Trent suddenly demanded. He stepped forward and looked into her dark blue eyes.

"Um . . . excuse me?" Laurie asked.

"You heard me."

Laurie sneered. They'd already been over this—

"You can't tell me, can you?" Trent asked. "Because she didn't do *anything*. You just built up some kind of ridiculous scenario in your mind. You just wanted to be

able to look yourself in the mirror, knowing that you'd screwed over a friend. It was *your* fault—"

"You're shouting, Trent." She swallowed and forced a laugh. Out of the corner of her eye she could see that everyone was staring at the two of them. He was embarrassing her now. He was putting on a show for their benefit. Well. It was time to end the entertainment portion of tonight's program. Immediately. "Why don't you just—"

"All Tina Vasquez ever did was try to be your friend," he snarled. "And you blew it. Just like you've blown every other friendship you've ever had." His voice dropped to a whisper. He leaned close to her. "Do you think that these people are really your friends, Laurie? Do you think they would be there for you if you really needed them? They're just scared of you. They know what happens if you get mad."

Laurie blinked hard. Her fists were clenched tightly at her sides. *No, no, no.* Those were all lies. First of all, Tina had tried to sabotage Laurie's rightful social status from the moment they met. If anything, Laurie had tried to be a friend to *Tina*. Second of all, Laurie had more friends than anyone she knew. Her house would be empty right now if she had no friends. Every single kid who mattered (and several who didn't) was here for one reason: Laurie Penrow *was* North Conroe.

"You know what's funny?" he said. "I just realized something. I always thought you were so popular. But that's not true at all. And for somebody who's supposedly such a loser, Tina has way more friends than you."

"I wouldn't *want* her friends," Laurie countered.

"Fine." He shrugged, then turned to the crowd. "Does anybody here really like Laurie Penrow?" he demanded.

Nobody answered.

Laurie's furious gaze swept the room.

Every pair of eyes was on the floor, or the wall, or the ceiling—anywhere but Laurie's face. Her stomach squeezed. Why were they doing this? Just because she had once been friends with Tina, because they saw that dumb old video, was that why they were all turning on her?

"I didn't think so," Trent stated in the silence. "But you don't want to say anything because nobody ever crosses Laurie Penrow. Well, you know what?" He turned to her and smiled. "I'm going to be the first."

She swallowed. She had to maintain control. He would not make her look weak. Never.

"What are you talking about, Trent?" she asked. "You're not making any sense."

"Here's something that'll make sense," he said. "As of now, we're finished. I'm dumping you." He cupped

his hands around his mouth and spun back toward the crowd. "You hear that, everyone? In front of all of you, I hereby dump Laurie Penrow."

Laurie shook her head violently. That was impossible. This whole night was impossible. She *couldn't* be dumped. This was her party, her scene . . . her world. Nobody could touch her. Not here.

"You can't," she said.

"Of course I can," he said calmly.

"Fine. Then get out, get off my property. You're nobody without me. You'll see—you're going to end up in that horrible military school now. I'm going to make sure of that."

Trent just shook his head at her. "You can't scare me anymore." He shoved his way back toward the door and disappeared.

Laurie laughed again. But the sound was empty. Everybody had turned their backs on her. They were all watching Trent leave.

Somebody will speak up, she promised herself. Her breath came fast. *Somebody will take my side. . . .*

Slowly, somberly, people began filing out of the stable.

Her pulse raced. Okay. This was fine. No problem. She nodded. People would forget about the video; it was only a few minutes that they saw, anyhow. And Tina

wasn't worth their time—she'd soon be forgotten, too. They could all go back to the pool and the game room and the stereo and pick up where they left off. Soon this nasty little incident would be a distant memory. Especially for Trent. In fact, he was probably kicking himself right now for being such a jerk in public. He would get about as far as the hot tub, and then he'd rush back to apologize. And she would even apologize to him.

Yes. She was *that* forgiving. All he had to do was turn around and come back. Then they would be together again. The way they were supposed to be.

Right?

Trent

After crisscrossing the winding roads near the Penrows' house for nearly an hour, Trent finally resigned himself to the fact that Tina was gone.

The night was very dark. She could have run anywhere by now. He only hoped that she'd called her mom to pick her up or that her friend Susan had been more lucky searching for her on foot. Of course, he hadn't seen Susan, either. . . .

The Jeep rolled to a stop at a lonely red light.

Trent drummed his fingers against the steering wheel.

What have I done?

He could have warned Tina about this a month ago. He could have warned her tonight. He could have, he could have . . . a hundred different possibilities whirled through his mind, and each one only made him feel worse. If only Susan hadn't been so hysterical when

chapter 17

she'd found him. He'd been sitting there, wallowing in solitude on the spiral staircase, when Susan came up out of nowhere and started yelling at him. A full five minutes passed before she mentioned that Tina and Laurie were at the stables. She kept firing off those accusations. . . . He barely understood what she was saying other than that he'd betrayed Tina in the worst possible way. Which was true. But if she'd told him—

Wait a second.

He shook his head, disgusted with himself. He was blaming Susan, wasn't he? He was blaming Tina's best friend. For *his* mistake. *She* hadn't plotted against Tina. Nope. Blaming Susan was something Laurie would do. There was only one person to blame for this entire nightmare.

Me.

The light turned green. He pressed his foot on the gas. The Jeep lurched forward. Tina's words to him at the beginning of the night still rang in his head: "This is all your doing. . . ." And she had been acting so cold, so removed. He had assumed she was just supernervous, but now he understood. She had already known about the plan by then. And she was giving him one last chance to come clean. She had been dropping hints like mad, now that he thought about it. She even mentioned the word *plan*. Trent felt like the biggest dolt on the planet. How could he have gone along with this? And why hadn't he just gone with his impulse at that moment to tell Tina the truth, to whisk her out of that fake party?

They could have celebrated her Sweet Sixteen in style somewhere else. An image flashed in his head of him and Tina at a fancy restaurant, her in that dress, looking over the table at him. . . . No. Now none of that would ever be his. Tina hated him now. And she was right to hate him. He had known, deep down, that Laurie was wrong. And he could have stopped her, even at the last minute. He should have *known* Laurie would use the stables for whatever prank she'd cooked up. She always conducted her illicit activities there. The stables were where they used to make out when they first started seeing each other. . . .

So what do I do now? he asked himself.

The lights of North Conroe glittered in the distance as he sped away from Laurie's neighborhood. They had never looked less inviting. It was as if a whole new life awaited him, one in which he was pretty much screwed. His friends had no doubt written him off as a nutcase. He could just picture Josh Frederick and the other guys on the basketball team as they talked about what he'd done. *"Dude! Can you believe that guy? He dumped*

Laurie Penrow! I knew something was wrong with him."

Whatever. If they had a problem with it, then they weren't his friends. He'd meant every word he'd said back at the stables. And he knew that a lot of people liked to hang out with him simply because it seemed like the right thing to do. He dated Laurie Penrow. They were scared of Laurie, so by extension they were scared of him.

It had nothing to do with real feelings.

Except in Tina's case . . .

He knew now that ruining his reputation was a small price to pay for breaking up with Laurie. He should have known it a long time ago. And now that he'd actually done it, he couldn't even remember why he had been so apprehensive. He felt liberated. He felt free. *That* was what mattered.

No . . . actually, what mattered was Tina. But somehow he always managed to forget that, didn't he? He always focused on himself—

Bee-bee-bee-bee-beep.

Trent frowned. What was that? His eyes flashed to the dashboard. It sounded like an alarm. But there was no warning light—

Bee-bee-bee-bee-beep.

The phone. Man. His father was probably calling to

ask him to fill the tank before he came home. He shook his head and picked it up.

"Hello?"

At first he couldn't hear anything but pounding, distorted music. He blinked. It definitely wasn't his father. For a delirious instant he thought Tina might have—

"Trent?" Laurie's voice blared out of the earpiece.

His jaw tightened. There was no point in talking to her. He said what he'd had to say. He dropped the phone back down on the seat. Why was she calling? Actually, he didn't even want to know the answer to that question; the past was behind him, and he refused to revisit it. He had to focus on the present. Right. His fingers trembled on the wheel. He'd made his decision.

Bee-bee-bee-bee-beep.

Laurie wasn't going to leave him alone. Of course not. That wasn't her style. She would force him to confront her.

Bee-bee—

He snatched up the phone again. "What?" he answered.

"Trent, listen to me," Laurie answered.

She sounded so plaintive. Almost desperate. But she was probably just trying to manipulate him. Everything was an act with her—*everything*. He shook his head. He

felt sick. How could he have ever allowed himself to fall under her spell? How could he have enjoyed putting on an act for Tina? By being phony? It was *despicable*.

Now that he thought about it, he was just like all the characters in *The Taming of the Shrew*. Everyone in that play pretended to be somebody else so they could get what they wanted.

Strange. Trent never thought he'd learn anything from Shakespeare. Weirder things had happened, though. He'd never thought he'd write a haiku, either. And he'd certainly never thought he'd want to sever all ties with Laurie.

"Trent?" Laurie asked. "Are you there?"

"We've got nothing to talk about," he said, sighing.

"Just come over, all right? We need to talk. I . . . I'm sorry. Okay? I—"

"It's too late for that, Laurie," he interrupted softly. "Good-bye." He hung up the phone again—only this time he pulled the phone out of the dash. Now he was unreachable—at least until he got home.

In a way he was glad she'd called.

Yes, with that brief exchange she'd helped him to come to an important realization: He hardly ever thought for himself. She was counting on him to obey her. She was counting on him to be passive.

Well, the old, passive Trent was long gone. And the new Trent was going to do anything—*anything*—to make amends with Tina for ruining her sixteenth birthday. Because he was starting to realize something else, too. Something that filled him with fear and regret and sadness all at once.

He'd been with the wrong girl all along. He'd started realizing the truth ever since that first day at LotsaFunland, but he'd tried so hard to deny it for Laurie's sake. And for his own. Laurie might have provided him with a quick fix to stay out of military school . . . but it was Tina who'd given him the tools to stay at North Conroe for good. She hadn't even done any of his work for him. She'd gotten him to appreciate Shakespeare—really *appreciate* it—using only her humor and kindness and infectious enthusiasm. Most of all, she'd gotten him to *think*. In all these months of going out with Laurie, he hadn't ever been able to say that about her.

So now he had to earn Tina's forgiveness. And he would, no matter what. At this point he had nothing left to lose. He wouldn't rest until he'd made up for his mistake.

Tina

chapter 18

"Well, just look on the bright side, Tina. At the very least, you ruined one of Laurie Penrow's parties. *That's* going to have people talking."

Tina groaned, pulling the covers over herself. She wished her tiny bed could just swallow her up. And she felt equally as bad for Susan. The poor girl had been sitting at Tina's desk all night, struggling for hours and hours just to get Tina to *smile*. But Tina didn't think she would ever be able to smile again. Or sleep, for that matter.

"And have I mentioned that you are the bravest person I know?" Susan asked.

"Only about a hundred times." Tina moaned.

"Well, you are. If I had been in your shoes—I mean, if I had found the video that Laurie made, I probably would have run home and hid under my bed. For a month. But you had the brains to turn the tables on them. To put Laurie Penrow in her place once and for all."

Susan and Tina had been going over the story all night, every detail: how Tina had found Laurie's mean video about her and realized what was really going on. How she had raced home, sobbing. Her first thought was to hide, actually. But instead she got the idea about the old video, the one showing her and Laurie as kids, back when Laurie wasn't the beauty she was now. Back when Laurie was just Laurie, her best friend—a little goofy looking but still a lot of fun. Tina didn't want to think about that time. Would she ever be able to remember the fun they'd had together as kids without wincing?

Sunlight was already streaming into her little bedroom. Tina turned her bleary eyes toward the window and caught a glimpse of the paperboy riding by on the street. *Jeez*. It was a new day. A new beginning. The prospect of getting up filled her with dread. But she couldn't hide in bed forever. She couldn't leave, either, though. She couldn't risk running into anyone who'd been at Laurie's last night. . . .

"You should have seen it," Susan went on. "I mean, I looked for you for like an hour or something, and by the time I came back, there were only, like, twenty people there. And Laurie was pleading with them not to go."

"I know," Tina said as gently as she could manage. "You told me that part already."

Susan laughed. "Oh yeah. Right. I guess I'm just a little punchy from lack of sleep."

Tina *was* grateful that Susan had tracked her down here and even more grateful that Susan had spent the night . . . but right now she would have preferred silence. Every part of her body seemed to ache—and that wasn't even counting the pain that had consumed her ever since she'd run out of the stables. She turned on her side, facing the desk. Her bones creaked.

"Well, did I tell you the part about how I screamed at Trent?" Susan asked. "He really felt terrible."

Tina sat up straight and nodded, trying her best just to muster a grin. But hearing Trent's name hurt too much.

"Maybe I should go home," Susan said. "I mean, I can—"

"No." Tina shook her head. She found herself yawning uncontrollably. "I mean, only if you want to. I want you to stay, but . . ."

"Then I'm staying," Susan stated. She giggled, then stopped herself. "Sorry—I don't mean to laugh. I don't know what my problem is. My brain feels funky. You know, I think this is my first all-nighter since the sixth grade."

Tina rubbed her eyes. "Did you stay up trying to console somebody that time, too?"

"Nope. I stayed up eating candy corns and watching horror movies. I was sick for a week."

Tina's hands fell to her lap. She frowned. She could just picture Susan doing that, staring at the flickering TV screen and stuffing candy into her face. . . . She chuckled. And for some reason, she couldn't stop. All of a sudden she was laughing uncontrollably. So was Susan. The laughter came from nowhere; she felt like a cartoon character—as if she'd been plugged into some kind of machine that momentarily erased the pain. Tears welled in her eyes. Her face turned red. Her sides started to hurt. . . .

"Hooray!" Susan cried. She threw her hands over her head. "I made you laugh!"

Finally, after what seemed like several minutes, Tina managed to take a deep breath.

She shook her head. "Wow," she croaked. "I see what you mean about feeling punchy."

"I'm just glad we don't have any candy corns," Susan joked.

Tina smiled at her. "Susan . . . you know, I never got a chance to say how sorry I was for being such a jerk to you this past month. I mean—"

"Don't worry about it," Susan interrupted. "I didn't handle it the best way, either."

"You *did*, though," Tina countered. "Because you were right. I was the stupid one. . . ." She hung her head. The pain was returning again. She couldn't even bear to *remember* how she had argued with Susan over Laurie and Trent.

"You weren't stupid, Tina," Susan soothed. "It has nothing to do with stupidity. Anybody in your position would have done the exact same thing. I'm just incredibly paranoid and suspicious. The sad thing is that I actually turn out to be right sometimes—" She drew in a quick breath.

Tina glanced up.

Susan's gaze was fixed to the window. Tina followed the direction of her eyes. *Oh my*—

A black Jeep was pulling up in front of her house.

Tina's heart bounced. She knew that Jeep. It was Trent's. . . .

"Is that . . . ?" Susan whispered, leaving the question hanging.

Yes. Trent stepped out of the driver's side onto the street. He was still wearing the same stained black T-shirt and ratty pair of jeans that he'd had on the night before. He actually looked like *he* hadn't slept, either.

Dark circles ringed his eyes. His face was drawn. He peered at the house, as if to make sure that this was really his intended destination, then pulled his knapsack out of the Jeep and slammed the door.

"It's *him!*" Susan whispered. She whirled to Tina. "What do you want to do?"

But Tina could only shake her head. Her heart was firing like a piston.

Trent slowly approached her front door.

"He must want to come in," she gasped. "I have to stop him. My mom will wake up." Quick as a flash, she leaped out of bed and dashed out of her room—down the narrow hall to the entranceway. She threw open the door just as he was lifting his finger to ring the bell.

His hand hung in midair for a moment. He stared at her through the screen.

She stared back, breathing heavily.

"I, uh . . . ," he began.

"I saw you coming," she whispered. "What do you want?"

"Can I come in?"

Tina swallowed. She glanced toward her room. Susan was standing outside her door, biting her lip, waiting.

"My mom will wake up," Tina said quietly, turning

back to him. She couldn't stand to make eye contact, so she kept her head down. "Just tell me what you want."

"I promise I'll be quiet," he insisted. "I just want to show you something...."

"I don't know, Trent—"

"It's your birthday present," he said.

Her chest tightened. "Didn't you give that to me last night?" she asked, still unable to meet his gaze. "The party, wasn't that your idea, too?"

"Please let me in, Tina," he begged. "I've really got to explain. I'm not going to leave. I'm just going to camp out on your lawn until you open the door."

Tina shook her head. She shot another quick glance down the hall. Susan tiptoed into the entranceway. She glanced blankly through the screen door at Trent.

"I think I'm gonna take off," Susan whispered.

For a moment Tina held her breath. Part of her desperately wanted Susan to stay. Part of her wanted the two of them to remain inside the safe cocoon of Tina's home until the next ice age. But another part wanted Trent to explain himself. And the sooner Tina learned the whole truth, the sooner she would be able to put Trent Rostand and Laurie Penrow behind her for good. She had to be strong. She couldn't hide forever.

Susan patted her shoulder and opened the screen door. "I'll see you later."

"Bye," Tina murmured.

Trent held open the door as Susan hurried past him. Susan paused briefly on the street and glanced over her shoulder. "Call me later!" she mouthed.

Tina nodded. Her eyes darted to Trent.

"So," he said. "Are you going to let me in?"

"You promise you'll keep your voice down?" she asked.

He raised his hand. "I swear."

"Okay." She stepped aside and gestured toward her room. "Come in. But make it short. I haven't slept yet."

"Neither have I," he said hoarsely. "How did you get home, by the way?"

She raised her eyebrows, then closed the door behind him. "I drove."

His mouth fell open. "You've got your license? But you didn't say anything. Hey, that's great—"

"Shhh," she whispered.

He seems genuinely happy for me, she thought. *Why does he even care?*

He hesitated. "Um . . . there's something I want to read to you. It's a haiku I wrote."

He had some nerve. Like the one his girlfriend had

written? Like the one on the tape they had wanted to use to humiliate her? A dam seemed to burst inside her, releasing a torrent of rage that flooded every vein in her body. "Why? Do you want to finish what you started back at Laurie's place—"

"No, no, no," he interrupted. His face went pale. He waved his hands quickly in denial. "It has nothing to do with Laurie. Well . . . not entirely."

Tina folded her arms in front of her chest. Not entirely. That was just great. What was *that* supposed to mean? And who did he think he was, barging in here with these cryptic riddles at six A.M.—after he had practically destroyed her the night before? Why had she even let him in the house? It was ridiculous. "Just go home, Trent," she found herself muttering. "I'm too tired for this."

"I just need a minute of your time," he said, and his voice was shaking. He swung the knapsack off his back and held it up to her as if that would somehow prove his sincerity. "If you let me show you this, you might start to understand."

"Understand *what?*"

He shook his head. He blinked rapidly. His lips trembled. "Just let me show you this," he whispered.

Tina studied his face, her heart still pounding. For all she knew, this was another prank. On the other

hand, it was six in the morning, and he *did* look desperate. And Susan had mentioned that he felt awful. Besides, resisting him now would only prolong the agony. He was already inside the door. She couldn't feel any worse. At the very least, nothing could surprise her anymore. Not after last night.

"I don't know why I'm doing this, but okay. Let's go into the den; maybe we won't wake my mom up in there," she finally relented, pointing toward the den.

He nodded, waiting for her to lead the way.

With a sigh she padded through a swinging door into the room. *Jeez.*

For some reason, as ridiculous as it was, she couldn't help but think about how unimpressive her house was compared to the Penrows' vast estate. Why? What did she care what Trent thought about her house? She was *proud* of it: the antique lamps, the overstuffed couch, even the wood paneling. Well, maybe not so much the wood paneling. Everything else, though.

But in a way, caring about that kind of stuff was symbolic of how this whole mess got started in the first place. Tina never used to think about such superficial things. Except when she was around Laurie Penrow.

Like last night, for instance. Perfect example. She'd spent all that time dressing up, obsessing about how she

looked. She'd been so concerned with impressing Laurie. Why? She was never concerned with impressing her *real* friends, like Susan. But since Laurie attached so much importance to appearances, Tina felt the need to dress up . . . to be someone else. To put on an act. Just the way Trent had . . .

But it was best not to think too hard about that. She'd wasted enough time on Trent already. On getting over him. On helping him. On *everything*.

"Have a seat," she said, waving her hand at the couch.

"Thanks." Trent sat down on the edge of the cushions and started rifling through the bag. She couldn't help but notice how *nervous* he was. His motions were so quick and jerky. It was pretty ironic. He almost reminded her of how nervous *she* was, back on that first day he walked into the classroom a month ago.

"Here it is." Trent finally dug a piece of paper out of the bottom of the bag.

She nodded. Whatever this was, it had better be quick. She was about to pass out from sleep deprivation. She flopped down on the couch—as far away from him as possible.

Trent sat up straight. Then, as if rethinking things, he actually got off the couch and knelt in front of Tina on the floor. Without meeting her eyes, he reached out and

took her hand. Tina held her breath. She wanted to yank her hand back, but she couldn't. It felt so good to touch him again. . . . No, she couldn't let herself think that way.

Trent took a deep breath and started reading from the piece of paper in his other hand. "'Portrait of the *Real* Loser.'"

He cleared his throat. The noise sounded small and nervous. "A haiku of apology, by Trent Rostand. 'I am so sorry . . . for everything I've done . . . won't you forgive me?' The end."

In spite of her anger and exhaustion, she had to smile a little. So he'd figured out a clever way to say he was sorry. Fine. *And* he was cute. She already knew that, though. But if he honestly thought that she would forgive him after a three-line poem, he was sadly mistaken. He would have to do a lot more than that. . . .

"Trent, who do you think you are, coming here like this, writing me poetry—"

But he cut her off. "'What am I, sir!'" he quoted. "'Nay, what are you, sir! O immortal gods . . .'"

She laughed out loud. This was really funny, actually. He was acting out one of the final scenes in *The Taming of the Shrew*—

"Hey, that was good!" she exclaimed before she could check herself.

"It's, um, sort of a work in progress," he mumbled. His face was flushed. He stared down at the rug. "Look, forget the Shakespeare. The point is . . . What I'm trying to show you with this birthday present . . ." He took a deep breath. "See, I was playing a role with you this past month. But it wasn't even the right role. Like the way all the characters played false roles in the play. You know?"

She nodded, amazed. She couldn't answer. A strange thought occurred to her: He'd paid attention to her in class. He'd actually learned something. And she was responsible for it. The summer wasn't a complete waste of time, was it?

"All those mornings I spent with you, starting with that trip to LotsaFunland, I convinced myself that I was just pretending to like you," he said. "I convinced myself that the whole thing was an act. That I was just going through these motions to earn a good grade." He lifted his gaze. "But then I realized something. I wasn't acting at all."

Tina simply stared back at him. The fogginess and exhaustion began to melt away. She found that her throat was clogged with a large, painful lump. Why was he telling her this? Didn't he realize that it was too late? She'd gotten over him. A long time ago. The very first time he ever set foot in that classroom. And she was certainly over him now . . .

"There's something more, too," he added, swallowing. "Right after you ran out of that party, I did something I should have done the moment I met you. I broke up with Laurie. For good. Because . . . because . . ." His voice grew so strained that he could barely speak. "Because I was falling for the girl I was supposed to be fooling."

Tina's eyes began to moisten. She'd thought she'd cried as much as humanly possible in the past ten hours. But apparently there were still some tears left. Only these tears didn't spring from shame or sadness. They sprang from some other place—a place she'd thought had been destroyed forever. She was aware of a specific emotion now, much like the elation she'd felt when she'd first grown comfortable with Trent—only it was far more powerful. She didn't even think it had a name.

"I guess what I'm saying is that I'm trying to give you a sign, Tina. A smile or a glance. Like in the haiku you wrote. Remember?"

"I remember," she said. The words were barely a whisper.

Still kneeling, he placed his hands on her knees. His eyes were so beautiful, glimmering in the morning sun: those eyes she knew so well—first from afar and then up close, day after day after day.

"Will you ever be able to forgive me?" he whispered.

"I don't know," she murmured.

"What can I do?"

"You can start being honest with me," she said.

"I will."

She bit her lip, frightened of what she was about to say. It had taken a lot of courage for Trent to do this. She knew that. And even though she was still angry and hurt, she knew that she had a confession to make if they were truly going to move past this.

"You know, Trent . . . I wasn't totally honest with you, either," she said. "The only reason I signed up to be your tutor was because I had a crush on you. And I know it was wrong. And that was why I never did anything about it—"

But before she could say another word, he leaned forward and planted a kiss on her lips.

It was so soft, like the stroke of a paintbrush—so unlike what she'd imagined her first kiss would be. No, it was far more subtle and magical. What surprised her the most was that she'd gotten it right in poetry: It was like a certain kind of glance. Or a special smile. It was something unique that could never be repeated.

And when she opened her eyes again, it was over.

A delicious shiver traveled throughout her entire

body as he leaned away from her. She shook her head. All she could think was: I've done it. I've finally done the impossible. I've kissed Trent Rostand.

"You *should* have done something about the crush you had," he said. "And I should have, too."

She smiled.

He laughed.

All of a sudden the two of them were cracking up.

"Shhh!" she tried to whisper, but it was useless. "My mom will wake up," she managed between giggles.

"Then let's get out of here," he said, hopping up and taking her hand. "There's one more part of your birthday present." He tugged her out of the sofa. Their fingers intertwined. "An all-expenses-paid day at LotsaFunland." With a flourish he pulled a long string of carnival tickets from his pocket.

She shook her head. "Um . . . Trent? LotsaFunland doesn't open for, like, four hours."

He shrugged. "Then we'll just have to drive around," he said. "Maybe you can tell me about *A Midsummer Night's Dream*. That's what I have to read next."

"Trent." She groaned.

"Just kidding." He leaned forward and kissed her again.

Tina and Trent

epilogue

LotsaFunland. Of course it would have to be at LotsaFunland.

They went out to breakfast at a diner and watched the sunrise. They talked for hours about everything, about nothing. And then, paying the bill, Trent flashed those LotsaFunland tickets in front of her again.

"You've got to be kidding—all I can think about is climbing into bed." She groaned. "I feel like I haven't slept in days."

"Me too, but there's one last part of your birthday gift I still have to give you."

"My birthday was yesterday. How about giving me the gift of a long nap instead?" She giggled. She couldn't believe she was standing here in a highway diner, on a beautiful summer Sunday morning, with the incredibly handsome Trent Rostand begging her to hang out with him.

"Nope, it's gotta be today." Then he added, "But I

promise to have you home and in your bed before noon, deal?"

It sounded so ridiculous, she had to laugh. "Sure, since I don't think you're going to take no for an answer, anyhow."

Trent took her hand, and they walked out to the Jeep. She was giddy, dizzy. Was it lack of sleep or something else, something bigger than that? She looked over at Trent in the driver's seat. This was more than sleep deprivation, she thought, taking in his stunning profile, the stubble on his cheeks, the way his light eyes held the road and then turned to look at her.

"Almost there," he said, taking her hand across the seat. He let go to shift gears as they neared the entrance to the amusement park. They were so early, no one else was there. A few cars were in the lot, but those probably belonged to employees. Trent quickly parked and hopped out, racing around her side of the Jeep to open the door for her.

"Nice service at this place," she said with a giggle.

"We aim to please," he countered. "This way, miss." He took her hand and led her into the park.

"Oh no, not The Wacky Shack! I can't take it on zero hours of sleep and two cups of coffee," Tina protested.

"Would I do that to you?" Trent asked, his eyes glittering.

Tina looked up and found herself in front of the Ferris wheel.

"Hey, Josh," Trent greeted the guy running the controls. "Thanks again for hooking me up with the tickets last night. And I'm sorry I had to wake up your whole family to get them."

"No problem, man, anything for true love." He pulled open the gate on one of the cars and motioned to Tina that she should get in.

She couldn't believe this was happening. Trent had mentioned that a friend of his worked at the theme park, but it had slipped her mind. Now it was clear that he had been very busy last night—writing that haiku, tracking her down, and also waking this poor guy up to get LotsaFunland tickets before the park opened. As soon as the park really did open, all the kids from school would probably be here today—there wasn't a lot else to do in North Conroe on a Sunday. And they would all see Trent and Tina together.

Tina looked over at him. He didn't seem embarrassed to be seen with her—quite the contrary. He was grinning at her as if he couldn't take his eyes off her. "Your carriage awaits," he said.

Tina stepped into the bucket seat, and Trent cozied in beside her. His friend closed the gate in front of them and winked. "Have a good ride," he said, stepping back over to the controls. The engine of the Ferris wheel whirred to life, and before they knew it, they were on top of the big wheel, looking out over their little town. The Ferris wheel stopped slowly, allowing them a few minutes to take in the view.

"Is this my other birthday present?" Tina asked, turning to Trent. "It's beautiful up here. I can't remember the last time I was on this ride."

"This isn't your present." Trent shifted so that he could look right into her eyes. "What I have to tell you is your present. I only hope you'll accept it."

Tina was staring at his handsome face when the thought came into her head. Yes, she could forgive him. She didn't have to tell him that now, but she knew it in her heart at this moment. Trent was a good person, and she wanted him in her life.

"Tina, did you hear me?" he asked, pulling her back to the present. "I said I love you. I'm not afraid to say it. I'll say it a hundred times. In fact, I want the whole world to know. That's why we're here." Trent stood up, rocking the car. "You hear that!" he hollered down. "I love Tina Vasquez! I love her!"

"Sit down—you're going to kill me on the happiest

day of my life," she yelled up at him, tugging him down beside her.

"So do you think you might forgive me someday?" Trent looked at her, his eyes so sincere, it broke her heart.

"I already have," she whispered, and sealed it with a kiss.

About the Author

Daniel Parker is the author of over twenty books for children and young adults. He lives in New York City with his wife, a dog, and a psychotic cat named Bootsie. He is a Leo. When he isn't writing, he is tirelessly traveling the world on a doomed mission to achieve rock-and-roll stardom. As of this date, his musical credits include the composition of bluegrass sound-track numbers for the film *The Grave* (starring a bloated Anthony Michael Hall) and a brief stint performing live rap music to baffled Filipino audiences in Hong Kong. Mr. Parker once worked in a cheese shop. He was fired.

OFFICIAL RULES:
HarperCollins *"M2M Sweet 16"* Atlantic Records Video Sweepstakes

1. **No Purchase Necessary. Sweepstakes ends August 31, 2000**

2. **How to enter:** Fill out official entry form, or download and print an entry form from either the "M2M Sweet 16" website at www.harperchildrens.com/sweet16 or the M2M website at www.m2monline.com, or type or legibly print your name, address, and age on an 8.5" x 11" piece of paper and mail to the following address: HarperCollins "M2M Sweet 16" Atlantic Records Video Sweepstakes, P.O. Box 8094, Grand Rapids, MN 55745-8094. Only one entry per person allowed. All entries must be received by U.S. Mail by August 31, 2000, and subsequent entries will be automatically disqualified. Entries must be original. Sponsors are not responsible for lost, late, misdirected, damaged, incomplete, illegible entries, postage due mail or for any computer, on-line, telephone, human error or technical difficulties that may occur.

3. **Who May Enter:** Sweepstakes open to legal U.S. residents ages 8-18 as of February 1, 2000. Employees, and members of families living in the same household of Sponsors, HarperCollins Publishers, Atlantic Records, 17th Street Productions, M2M, their respective parent companies, subsidiaries, affiliates, divisions, franchises, advertising and promotion agencies, agents, fulfillment companies, retail licensees, printers, distributors and mailers are not eligible to enter Sweepstakes.

4. **Prizes: (1) Grand Prize:** Approximate Retail Value: $4,000. Travel prize includes round trip coach airfare for 3 days, 2 nights for winner and one parent/legal guardian to the taping location of an Atlantic Records music video in either New York, NY or Los Angeles, CA. Prize and travel will be scheduled within 6 months of winner selection. Sponsor chosen airline beginning and ending at the major U.S. airport closest to the winner's residence, standard hotel accommodations for 3 days and 2 nights (double occupancy). Ground transportation, meals, travel documents, travel insurance, medical insurance, taxes, gratuities, personal expenses and other expenses not specified herein are the sole responsibility of the winner. Ticketing must occur no less than 30 days prior to date of departure and is subject to availability and certain blackout dates and restrictions. Winner and parent/legal guardian must all travel together. Sponsor reserves the right to structure travel routes and hotel and hotel selection at its sole discretion. ARV for travel prize is approximate and may vary due to point of departure and fare fluctuations.

[Every attempt will be made to include the winner in the location and filming of an Atlantic Records music video. Final editing and selection is left to the sole discretion of Atlantic Records, its employees and their creative discretion. No guarantee is given or implied that the winner will participate in the making of the video or that the winner will be included in the final version of the music video.]

Fifty (50) Second Prizes: Approximate Retail Value: $850. Fifty first-place prize winners will be chosen at random to receive a copy of M2M's musical CD "Don't Say You Love Me."

All prizes will be awarded. Prizes are non-transferable; no prize substitutions of cash values of prizes allowed except at the discretion of Sponsor. All taxes are the responsibility of the winner(s) or their parent/legal guardian. All other expenses not specified herein are the sole responsibility of the winner.

5. **Drawing:** Drawing conducted on/about September 30, 2000 by an independent judging agency, whose decisions are final on all matters related to this Sweepstakes. Winning entries will be selected randomly. Odds of winning will vary depending on the number of entries received.

6. **Other Conditions:** Winner will be notified by mail by December 31, 2000. Winner must claim prize by returning an affidavit of eligibility, waiver of liability, travel and publicity release executed by them and their parent/legal guardian within 21 days from the date of notification or winner will forfeit prize. Winners consent to the use of their names and likenesses for advertising and promotional purposes without further compensation except where prohibited by law. By participating, each entrant agrees to abide by and be bound by these Official Rules. Sponsor reserves the right to substitute prizes of equivalent value if any prize listed becomes unavailable. All entries submitted become the property of the Sponsor and will not be returned. Sweepstakes void in Puerto Rico and wherever else prohibited by law.

7. **Winners List:** To receive a list of winners of prizes, send a stamped, self-addressed envelope before February 28, 2001 to HarperCollins "M2M Sweet 16" Atlantic Records Video Sweepstakes, P.O. Box 8004, Grand Rapids, MN 55745-8004. Winners lists available after March 31, 2001.

8. **Sponsors:** HarperCollins Publishing Company; Atlantic Records.

Enter the HarperCollins *"M2M Sweet 16"* Atlantic Records Video Sweepstakes

Name: _____

Address: _____

City: _____

State: _____ **Zip:** _____

Grade: _____ **Phone No.:** _____

HarperTrophy®
A Division of HarperCollins*Publishers*